Also by Jean Ure

Skinny Melon and Me
Becky Bananas, This is Your Life!
Fruit and Nutcase
The Secret Life of Sally Tomato*
Family Fan Club
Collins Book of Ballet and Dance Stories (ed.)

and for younger readers

The Monster in the Mirror
Big Tom
The Puppy Present

the Chums series

Buster
Bonnie
Bella
Bouncer

*also available on tape, read by John Pickard

Boys on the Brain

JEAN URE

Illustrated by Karen Donnelly

An imprint of HarperCollinsPublishers

First published in Great Britain by Collins 2001
Collins is an imprint of HarperCollins*Publishers* Ltd
77-85 Fulham Palace Road, Hammersmith,
London W6 8JB

The HarperCollins website address is: www.**fire**and**water**.com

1 3 5 7 9 8 6 4 2

Text copyright © Jean Ure 2001
Illustrations by Karen Donnelly 2001

ISBN 0 00 765788 9

The author and illustrator assert the moral right to be
identified as the author and illustrator of the work.

Printed and bound in Great Britain by
Bookmarque Ltd, Croydon, Surrey

For Eleanor Warren,
who writes wonderful letters

Tuesday

(1st day of winter term)

Honestly! Mum is impossible. She is obsessed with boys. She has boys on the brain.

First thing she says to me, over tea: "Guess who I travelled in with this morning? Brad Sullivan!"

Not, "How was school?" or "Who's your new class teacher?" or "What's your timetable like?" but Brad Sullivan.

"He's turning into a really nice boy," said Mum.

I felt like saying, "Feel free! He's all yours!" But Mum has such rotten taste in men she might just take me at my word. My mum and Brad Sullivan! I can just see it. And then, what about poor old Harry? He'd be out on his elbow.

On the whole I do feel that Harry is a Good Thing. The first decent bloke she's ever had. I wouldn't want her ditching him. So I restrained my worst impulses and said, "Really?" in a polite but yawny sort of way, hoping that she would get the message. The message being that *I do not want to hear about Brad Sullivan*. Or about any other boy, come to that. I am sick of the whole subject!

Instead, I tried talking about school. I said, "I'm so relieved! Me and Pilch are both in 9C." I've been worried, just lately, that they might split us up. "We're together for almost everything," I said. "Oh, and we've got Mrs Adey for English again!"

"Have you!" said Mum. "That's good!"

To be fair to her, she did try to take an interest, but in the end temptation overcame her. As usual! The opposite sex just dra-a-a-aws Mum like a magnet.

"Brad was telling me," (she goes) "how he's joined this new youth thing. They're going to put on musicals."

Meaning, in Mumspeak, why don't you join the youth thing? Join the youth thing and meet some boys!

"They're going to do a rock panto for Christmas," chirrups Mum.

"Wow," says I.

"They're desperate for female voices!"

Mum is *so* transparent.

"You can sing," she says. "Why don't you try joining?"

I said, "Because I have a voice like a corn-crake."

"No, you haven't!" said Mum. "You've got quite a nice voice."

"Pilch is the one who can sing," I said.

Of course, she jumped on this *immediately*.

"So you can both join!"

"Mum!" I yelled. "I haven't got time!"

She's always doing this to me. I wish she wouldn't! I know she means well. I know she only has my interests at heart. What she considers to be my interests. But I wish she would just leave me alone!

"You know what they say," sighed Mum. "All work and no play…"

I happen to like work. In any case, you have to study if you're going to get anywhere. And I am going to get somewhere! I am absolutely determined.

I said this to Mum and she said, "Oh, Cresta, you're so focused!"

I'm still trying to work out what she meant. Like, did she mean "I'm so lucky to have a 14-year-old daughter who thinks of something other than boys and clothes and make-up"? Or did she mean, "I wish I had a 14-year-old daughter that was a bit more like other people's 14-year-old daughters"?

I think that is what she meant. I think what she would really like is for me to be all dizzy and dumb. Well, maybe not dumb, exactly; but if we could have these cosy conversations about women's magazine type stuff. A hundred different ways to do your hair, or how to get your man in six easy lessons. That kind of thing.

I know I'm a disappointment to her, but I can only be how I am. And how I am is *me*. I wish Mum could accept that!

Harry the Hunk came round this evening and he and Mum went to the pub. Mum wanted to know what I was going to do. I said, "Oh, I'll probably get on with my homework."

Harry said, "Homework on a Friday? You're keen!"

"Oh, she is," said Mum. She said it kind of... wistfully.

"I've got simply stacks," I said.

I haven't, actually; it's too early in the term. What it was, I'd had this thought about Carlito and I wanted to write it down to read to Pilch tomorrow. I have thoughts about Carlito almost every night! Sometimes I find it hard to remember that he is only a figment of my imagination and not a real person. I only hope I never have to have an anaesthetic as I dread to think what kind of stuff I might start splurging on about as I come round!!! How embarrassing! Some of the things that go on in my head...

This latest thought, I am glad to say, is perfectly respectable. It came to me in bed, as thoughts so often do. (Bed is a good place for having thoughts.) It started with the discovery that Carlito cannot read or write, and just went on from there. This whole scene unrolled itself in my head. Pilch is bound to shriek "What?" And then when she has got over her shock she will instantly demand to know "Why?" and I will have no answer for her. I have no idea why! It is just something that happened.

It is a bit weird, in a way, since I am sure that in real life I would find it extremely difficult to converse with someone that was unable to read or write. Whatever would we talk about??? I think what it is, I think it is the Heathcliff factor. Like last term when we were reading *Wuthering Heights*, Mrs Adey said that Heathcliff represented a "primitive force". Carlito is a primitive force!

Boys like Brad Sullivan simply pale into insignificance. This is something Mum couldn't even begin to understand. The power of the imagination!

What I pictured was this sultry scene in a Spanish night club, where Carlito has gone with a party of his friends. One of them, who is secretly jealous of Carlito's smouldering good looks and the way he can have any girl he wants, tricks him into somehow revealing the fact that he cannot read. (Not yet sure how. I shall have to work this out!) The so-called friend, who is English and not very attractive, sneers in a superior way, thinking the rest of the party will also sneer and that the girls will no longer find him attractive, Carlito I mean, but of course they do.

Carlito himself is not in the least bit abashed. As Harry would say, in his coarse earthy way, "He doesn't give a monkey's!" This is on account of his wild gypsy blood, being very proud and fiery. He simply tosses his head and snarls –

I am not sure what he snarls! Something rude in Spanish. I wish I knew something rude in Spanish!

All I can think of is "Tu madre!" which I read somewhere is swearing, though I don't quite see how it can be since all it means is "your mother". But it sounds good. In Spanish!

At any rate it will have to do for now. Perhaps later I will think of something better.

Mum and Harry came back from the pub last night with some friends they had met. They sat up for simply hours shrieking and talking and playing music very loudly, so that in the end I had to go downstairs and ask them if they would mind being a bit quiet as I was trying to sleep.

"It is gone midnight," I said.

They seemed for some reason to think this was funny. But they did at least turn the music down.

Went into town after lunch and met Pilch. We mooched round the shops, ending up in Paperback Parade where we each bought a book. I bought *War and Peace* by Leo Tolstoy, and Pilch bought *Anna Karenina*, also by Tolstoy. We have made a vow to read them! *War and Peace* has almost fifteen hundred pages. One thousand four hundred and eighty-five, to be precise. Gulp! But last term Mrs Adey said it was a great book, so I am sure it will be interesting.

Bumped into Cindy Williams and Tasha Lansmann in the shopping centre. They were with boys. They are a bit like Mum: boys are all they ever think about. Cindy has put white stripes in her hair. She looks like a zebra crossing.

Told Pilch about Mum trying to get me to join the youth thing, just because of Brad Sullivan, and Pilch said her mum is the same. I don't see how she can be! Pilch's mum isn't man-mad. I said this to Pilch and she said, "No, but my sister is and in some ways that is even worse."

She said that Janine spends all her time, practically, in front of the mirror practising make-up and how to look flirty.

"And she's only twelve years old! It makes you feel like you're abnormal, or something."

"It's surely not abnormal," I said, "to want to get somewhere?"

I reminded Pilch of our pact that we made last term. Our sacred, solemn pact to foreswear the opposite sex until we have taken our A-levels and got to uni.

"It's the only way," I said.

Pilch sighed. She said, "Yes, I know."

"I mean, if we're going to be brain surgeons – "

I said this to cheer her up and bring a smile to her face. Becoming brain surgeons was what we always used to say when people asked us. We didn't mean it literally. It was just, like, a symbol of our determination to go places. To get somewhere. To be someone. Probably, in my case, a great writer, or maybe a TV journalist. I still haven't made up my mind. Neither has Pilch. Sometimes she thinks she'll be an architect, building glass bubbles and upsetting Prince Charles, other times she thinks she'll be an archaeologist, digging up lost civilisations. But anyway, something. We are not just going to be cogs! We are certainly not going to be like our mums.

After shopping we went back to Pilch's place and locked ourselves in her bedroom (away from her little brother) and read each other our latest episodes. My one about Carlito, Pilch's about Alastair.

Pilch's was in-ter-min-able! She has now decided that Alastair's parents are hugely noble and live in a castle somewhere in the Highlands of Scotland. She's got this book all about clans and she's written pages and pages describing in excruciating detail the tartans that people are wearing. She seems to think that men in kilts are sexy. She's even got Alastair wearing one! Blue and green, the clan of Mackenzie. He keeps saying things like "Och ay the noo", which I thought was a bit odd considering that last week she said he was speaking in "very cultured English". She explained, however, that when he's back home in the Highlands (or Heelands, as she calls them) he goes all Scottish and speaks "in a soft lilt".

Hm!

I didn't say anything, as it obviously turns her on.

After Pilch had read her bit, I read mine about Carlito in the night club. Pilch kept going *What?* just as I'd known she would. I told her to shut up and listen. After all, I hadn't gone "What?" about all that tartan stuff, and this was far more inspired! I'd pictured the whole scene. Carlito sitting there all smouldering and sultry and this pale geeky English type believing himself to be so-o-o-o superior and everyone thinking he's just dross. I'd written how Carlito curls his lip and goes "Tu madre!" with the candlelight glinting in his jet black hair.

All Pilch could think to say was, "What's he going on about his mother for?"

Honestly. I bet people didn't ask Tolstoy things like that!

I am writing this in the evening. Mum and Harry are downstairs watching telly. They asked me if I was going to stay and watch with them, but I said I'd got to make a start on *War and Peace*.

"It's nearly fifteen hundred pages," I said.

Harry then made one of his coarse earthy remarks which is totally unprintable. Four-letter words just spew out of that man! It is simply no use trying to impress him. Or Mum. I don't know why I bother.

Anyway, I don't really think they'd want me there with them. They're still at the stage of snogging on the sofa. I nearly caught them at it the other day.

I swear I heard this slurping noise as they prised their lips apart. I cannot see the attraction! I could if it were Carlito. But that is another matter…

Managed twenty pages of *War and Peace* last night. It is rather hard to get into, but I suppose that's because it is a classic. Classics are not meant to be easy. Anyone could read them if they were.

Harry the Hunk seems to have become a permanent weekend fixture. He stayed overnight on Friday and was still here this morning. And I don't think he sleeps on the sofa. Mum used to pretend that he did. She used to make this big production out of lugging bedclothes downstairs and saying how inconvenient it was living in a two-bedroom terrace and not having a spare room. But I used to lie awake and hear the stairs creaking, so I'm sure it was just for show. Now he's, like, here every weekend, all weekend, Friday night till Monday morning.

I'm not sure how I feel about this. OK, I guess. I mean, if it makes Mum happy. She's had lots of boyfriends over the years. Most of them have been dire; some of them have made her cry. And they've all regarded me as a definite impediment. Like, "Oh, that horrible spotty snot-nosed brat."

Harry just accepts me, like I am trying very hard to just accept him. It is not always easy, as I said to Pilch. It is all right for her, as she is used to living with a man, i.e. her dad. But when you are not accustomed to having a great hairy male about the place there are certain things that you have to try and remember. Like for instance you cannot just leave your underwear and stuff dripping over the bath. Well, I mean, you can. You could. It's not like there are any rules about it. But then I would feel embarrassed, and it is the same with the loo. To think that you are sitting where a male bum has been sitting. Not that there is anything very much that you can do about it, unless you carry your own portable loo seat with you.

Pilch giggles when I say this, but I am serious! It is a big intrusion into one's life. However, I will accept it for Mum's sake. She is obviously one of those women who needs a man to make her feel complete, and it is probably too late for her to change now.

But just imagine! If she didn't spend all that time snogging on the sofa she could be educating herself. She could be going to evening classes! She could be taking an OU course! She could be doing almost anything. And then instead of just being a bank clerk, she could be the actual manager!

I did once suggest this to her, but she said, "I cannot think of anything more boring!"

It is strange how different Mum and me are. I have this burning ambition, while Mum, it seems, is content with her lot. All she asks is a man in her life. And now she has one! So I must be happy for her and not worry about trivial things such as lavatory seats.

(2nd Week)

Pilch rang last night. It was almost half-past eleven, so I thought it must be one of Mum's friends. They are always ringing at these weird hours. They are a pretty weird bunch of people. Always shrieking and giggling. They don't act their age at all. But Mum seems to think they are amusing.

Anyway, it wasn't one of Mum's friends. Harry came

back from the hall and said, "There's a fish on the phone."

"A what?" said Mum.

Harry said, "A fish of some kind. It wants to speak to another fish."

"Oh, you mean Pilch," I said.

It was his idea of a joke. He knows perfectly well that we call each other Pilch. We have done for years. I remember the day we started doing it. It was when we were really young, like nine or ten, and we had this simply humungous row, and Pilch yelled, "You look like a stupid pilchard!" To which, with immense wit, I instantly retorted, "So do you… you… pilchard!" And we have called each other Pilch ever since.

Rather silly, really, but these things stick. I expect we will still call each other Pilch when we are middle-aged. Sometimes I forget that Pilch is really Charlie. Well, Charlotte, actually, but no one ever calls her that.

So anyway I charged out to the phone and said, "Why are you ringing me at this time of night?" I mean, it is practically unheard of. People simply do not do that sort of thing in Pilch's house. Unlike Mum and Harry, who behave like teenagers, Pilch's mum and dad go to bed at reasonable grown-up type hours. Pilch says they are always safely snoozing by eleven o'clock. That is what grown-ups ought to do. Not sit around playing loud music and keeping their children awake till after midnight.

"I wanted to tell you," said Pilch. "I've found some more swear words for you. For Carlito. He could say... caramba."

I said "What?"

"Caramba," said Pilch.

I asked her what it meant and she said she didn't know, but she thought it had to be swearing of some kind. She had just read it in a book.

"In *Anna Karenina*?" I said, somewhat surprised.

Pilch said, "Well – n-no. Not in *Anna Karenina*. I'm not actually reading that just at present."

I said, "Why not?"

"I've read nearly a whole chapter!" said Pilch. "How much have you read?"

"More than you," I said.

It's true. I have now reached page 55! (It is still rather difficult, but I think maybe this is because the print is so small.)

When I went back to the kitchen, Mum and Harry were grappling with each other over by the cooker. They broke apart in a guilty fashion as I came in. I felt like saying, "Please don't mind me. I realise that you are in the throes of sexual passion."

Tasha Lansmann said today that she thinks Mrs Pritchard is having an affair with Mr Bunting. She said that she bumped into Mr Bunting coming out of the library, and that he looked decidedly shifty and was "adjusting his dress". This is such a disgusting expression! All it means is fiddling with his flies. And it is probably quite untrue. He probably just had an itch in an embarrassing place. Tasha Lansmann sees sex everywhere. All the same, I shall look at Mrs Pritchard most carefully next time I go to the library. These things do happen.

Something intensely annoying. At lunch time me and Pilch had gone to the loo when suddenly there was the sound of the door crashing open and feet clumping in, and it was Cindy Williams and Tasha Lansmann. I could tell it was them by their loud squawking voices.

"So who are you asking?" goes Tasha. "You asking Mel and her crowd?"

Cindy says yes, she's asking practically everybody. "I want it to be a real rave, you know?"

She's talking about her birthday party.

"Boys?" says Tasha.

At which Cindy sniggers and says, "What do you think?"

So then they have a bit of a giggling session, then Tasha goes, "What about Ticky and Tocky?" And I freeze, 'cos this is a name they've recently invented for me and Pilch.

"You must be joking!" goes Cindy. "That pair? They'd put the kiss of death on anything, they would!"

Personally I wouldn't go to Cindy's rotten party if she fell on her bended knees and begged me, and Pilch says that she wouldn't, either. All the same, it just goes to show that you cannot be even the teeniest, tiniest bit different without being reviled and cast out. As Harry said the other day, when Mum was going on about the government, "It was ever thus." Not that that is much comfort.

I just hope they haven't upset Pilch. She is very sensitive.

Have reached chapter five of *War and Peace*. The trouble with very thick paperbacks is that you can't open them wide enough to read the left-hand side of the page properly. It is quite tiresome. But I am going to persist because after all it is a classic.

Went to the library to look at Mrs Pritchard. Also to see if there was a copy of *War and Peace* that I could borrow that might be easier to read than the one I bought, but there wasn't so I took out Harry Potter, instead. I am not giving up on *War and Peace*, but I have come to the conclusion that a diet of nothing but classics is probably a bit indigestible, especially when they are in small print and you cannot read properly on the left-hand side of the page.

Looked hard at Mrs Pritchard but couldn't see any signs that she was any different from usual, which I think there would be if she were having an affair with Mr Bunting. Whenever Mum takes up with a new bloke it's like total meltdown. She goes all moony and giggly and starts wearing these utterly unsuitable clothes. Crop tops and miniskirts and stuff that makes me really ashamed to be seen with her. Mrs Pritchard wasn't in the least bit moony or giggly, she was quite sharp and spiky, the same as always. So I think Tasha was just fantasising.

In any case, it would be entirely too trivial. I mean, Mrs Pritchard is a librarian. She has better things to do with her time. I know Mr Bunting is generally reckoned to be quite hunky, like he has these muscles all bulging out of his arms like waterlogged balloons, and people such as Cindy and Tasha hang around and gawp when he goes running in his shorts. But he teaches geography and has a brain the size of a pea. He is totally illiterate. He once gave me C minus for my geography homework and wrote "Its not good enough Cresta." *Its* instead of *It's*. And no comma! How could Mrs Pritchard have an affair with a man like that?

I hate geography, anyway.

Thursday

Pilch came into school today very upset as her mum suggested to her last night that maybe she should go on a diet. Pur-lease! Has her mum never heard of anorexia? It is true that Pilch is a bit on the plump side, but so what? That is the way she is made. It is the way she is happy. Why should she go and change her natural basic shape just to satisfy her mum?

Pilch said gloomily that it's because of her sister being thin as a pin and going out with all these boys, even though she is only twelve and a half.

"Mum thinks I'm being left behind."

"So she wants you to starve yourself?" I said.

Honestly! What with my mum going on about boys, and now Pilch's mum wanting her to starve herself, it's a wonder we're not both on Prozac.

Pilch said anxiously, "You don't think I'm fat, do you?"

I said, "No, you're just well covered, and even if you were fat, what would it matter?"

"I wouldn't want to be fat," said Pilch.

I said, "Now you're just being sizeist! You're as bad as your mum."

Pilch said it was all very well for me as I am what she calls "a fashionable shape". In other words, thin. I said, "That just happens to be the way that nature made me," and I got on my high horse a bit and started lecturing her about turning herself into a media creation.

Pilch said, "What do you mean, a media creation?"

"Like you read about in the papers," I said.

I told her that I was sick of young people always being depicted as lame-brained airheads only interested in the opposite sex, head-banging music, designer drugs and clothes.

"Some of us have a bit more going for us than that! We don't spend all our time gazing into mirrors and tarting ourselves up and going on diets and making ourselves ill. Your mum ought to be ashamed of herself," I said.

Pilch cheered up a bit when I said this. She confessed that she had lain awake half the night pinching bits of flesh between her finger and thumb and wondering whether she ought to give up eating entirely, or at any rate stick to yoghurt and raw carrots.

"It was making me really miserable," she said, as we stood in the queue for lunch. "And oh, look!" she added. "They've got macaroni cheese!"

I don't really like macaroni cheese that much but I ate some just to keep her company. I think it is important that we stand shoulder to shoulder in this crisis.

Harry came round. As usual. He and Mum went up to the pub. Also as usual. Mum said, "You don't mind, Cresta, do you?"

I said, "Why should I mind?"

"Well – " Mum looked at Harry. This sort of "Help me!" look. "It seems so awful! Me going out to enjoy myself while you just mope here with a book."

"I'm perfectly happy," I said.

"Yes, I know," said Mum, "but—"

"You ought to get out more," said Harry.

I said, "I do get out! I go to school every day. Or hadn't you noticed?"

"There's no need to be rude," said Mum.

I wasn't being rude. But I hate it when they start on at me like I'm some kind of freak! Is it truly so abnormal to want to get somewhere in life? You'd think with all the bad experience Mum has had she would be pleased I don't gad about, as Nan would say.

Maybe she is scared that I am a lesbian, though what there is to be scared about I really don't know. It is perfectly acceptable. But anyway, I'm not! If Carlito were to suddenly appear I would gad like crazy. I wouldn't be able to stop myself! I would do all kinds of unspeakable things. I would snog, I would French kiss, I would probably even have under-age sex… Gulp! It is probably just as well that he is merely a figment of my imagination.

"So! You really don't feel like joining us?" said Mum.

"Truly," I said. "I have things to do."

"Well, all right. We shan't be late," said Mum. "We'll probably all come back here."

"Yes, and this time," said Harry, "the nasty old folk will behave themselves. No noise! That's a promise!"

They're back here, now. I'm in my room and they're downstairs, and they are making a noise. It seems they can't help it. They're playing music VERY LOUD. But I don't want to be laughed at again so I've just stuffed cotton wool in my ears and am doing my best to ignore it.

It is not easy.

Saturday

Met Pilch in the shopping centre. Bumped into Tasha, on her own, i.e. without Cindy. But with a boy. The boy was Brad Sullivan. So much for Mum's plan for him and me to get together. Ha! I didn't want to, anyway. But it intensely annoyed me when Pilch said, "Wow! Where did she get that from?"

I said, "It's only Brad Sullivan. He lives in my road."

"Oh! He's the one your mum wanted you to meet," said Pilch.

"I don't need to meet him," I said. "I've already met him. I know him." Well, I do, sort of. We always say hello.

"He's kind of cute," said Pilch.

Cute??? Brad Sullivan??? No way!

"He reminds me of Carlito," said Pilch.

Indignantly I said, "He isn't anything like Carlito!"

Pilch said, "I think he is."

"Well, you can think what you like," I said, "but he's not your character, so how would you know?"

She said, "I'm just going by the way you describe him."

"Well! Ho!" I said. "If I were going by the way you describe Alastair I would think he was a total nerd."

Pilch's face suddenly transmuted into this big over-ripe tomato.

"What do you mean?" she said, all tight and quivering.

"Tall and willowy, lissom of limb and lithe of body, with hair like spun sunshine." That is, actually, what she wrote. It was so naff that I memorised it. "Anyway," I said, "if he's Scotch he's a Celt, and Celts don't look like that."

"Oh?" said Pilch. "So what do they look like, according to you?"

40

I said, "I know what they look like… short and dark and squat."

That shut her up! I know it was mean, destroying someone's fantasy, but it served her right for saying that that stupid Brad Sullivan looked like Carlito. She didn't talk to me again for another five minutes, until this woman came over to us wanting us to give money for cancer research and we wouldn't because we once read somewhere that they torture animals, and the woman said, "Suppose you got cancer?" to which Pilch replied, "A principle is still a principle," which I thought was rather good, and that got us talking again. Me and Pilch never stop talking for very long. We have too much to say to each other!

Mum complains about it, because of the telephone bill. She says, "How you can be at school together all day and then gabble on for hours in the evening, I really do not know."

It is because we have things to discuss. Important things. School things, work things, book things. Things about Alastair and Carlito! Pilch and I have always talked. Back in Year 7 Ms Martin used to say, "Cresta McMorris and Charlotte Peake. I want you at opposite sides of the room." But even then we used to pass notes!

And then we had our secret language that no one but us could understand. IBBY language. We used to put an Ib after the first letter of every word – unless it began with a vowel, in which case we put an N in front of it. Verree complicated! But we got so's we could rattle it off.

That was when we were in Juniors. I can't do it now. Unfortunately. If I could, I would go up to Cindy and Tasha and yell, "Sibtupid miborons!" And I'd do a rude gesture to go with it.

Came back here with Pilch to read our latest episodes and found the whole place pulsating.

"Oh, God," I said, "they're at it again!"

"At what?" said Pilch.

I said, "Playing their music!"

As soon as me and Pilch appeared, Harry very ostentatiously turned the volume down.

"Sorry," he said. He put a finger to his lips. "Old folk being noisy again!"

"What is it?" said Pilch.

Mum, foolishly beaming, said, "They were my favourite group when I was young." She held out a record sleeve. She has become a real vinyl nut since meeting Harry. It seems CDs aren't loud enough, or something. "Look!"

Pilch took the sleeve with this air of naïve wonderment.

"It's a record," she said.

"I know! Isn't it brilliant?" said Mum. "This album came out on my sixteenth birthday!"

"And it's still playable," said Harry. "Who said records don't last?"

Pilch was staring, like, transfixed, at the sleeve. It was green and purple, with swirly bits.

She said, "Dawn of Humanity... is that the name of the group or of the album?"

"You've got to be kidding me!" said Harry.

"It's the name of the group," said Mum. She snatched back her precious sleeve. "Please don't tell me you've never heard of them!"

"Mum," I said, "things have moved on."

Mum sniffed. A bit huffy. "Fat lot you'd know about it," she said. "Spend your life with your head buried in a book."

I grumbled to Pilch as we came upstairs.

"It's horrible," I said. "They play it all the time."

"I think it's fun," said Pilch.

"You wouldn't," I told her, "if you were trying to read *War and Peace*."

Pilch said she didn't expect, if she were trying to read

War and Peace, she would find anything much fun.

"They're really hard going, aren't they?" she said. "These Russian things?"

"They're classics," I said.

"Yes, I know," said Pilch; and she heaved this big sigh.

Pilch worries me sometimes. She doesn't seem as committed as she used to be. I know it was my idea that we should read the classics, but she agreed with me. I didn't force her. I just felt we ought to tackle something a bit – well! Worthy. Of course I have already done *Jane Eyre* and *Pride and Prejudice*; Pilch has only seen them on the telly. *Anna Karenina* is the first classic she has ever tackled.

Maybe she just needs a bit of a breathing space. I am not going to nag as I feel that would be counter-productive. I will just wait and see what happens.

Drove over to Wimbledon Dog Track with Mum and Harry. Not, alas, to see greyhounds but to look for vinyl at this record fair that's held there.

Record fairs, it seems, are full of the weirdest people! Strange anoraky men clutching big bags and long lists of the stuff they're looking for. They speak in these nerdy, high-pitched voices and they loom over you and breathe over you as you go through the records. And when they find one they think they might want, they take it out of its sleeve and hold it up to the light and peer at it this way and that way, sometimes through a magnifying glass. If they discover even the tiniest mark, totally invisible to the naked eye, they point it out, with great earnestness, to the person that's selling it.

"Look at this," they go, in their nerdy flutey voices. "There's a mark about half a centimetre in. Can you see it? Just there, where my finger is... is it fly doings, or is it a scratch?"

I didn't know that flies did things on records but apparently they do. And then it sticks and causes the needle to go thunk or to fly into the air.

I looked in vain, amongst all the anorakys, for anyone resembling Carlito. I look for boys who look like Carlito everywhere I go! They are very rare in this part of the world, though I did see a pizza delivery boy the other day who looked like him from a distance, only when I got close he turned out to be all nerdy and spotty. A big disappointment! But I live in hope.

Mum, meanwhile, lives in hope of finding this one particular album called Driftwood.

"If you come across it," she told me, "buy it! No matter what the price."

She gave me some money and sent me off, but I didn't find it, and nor did she or Harry. I looked ever so hard! I mean, I do like to make her happy if I can. I waded through stacks and stacks of grungy old fly-spattered records, but it wasn't there.

"What's so special about it, anyway?" I said.

"It's part of my youth," said Mum. "Just imagine, Cresta! You're missing out on so much! You won't have anything to look back and remember when you're my age."

Oh, yes, I shall! I shall remember reading *War and Peace*.

I am now on page one hundred and forty-three.

Phew!

Monday

(3rd week)

Mum said to me over tea, "Harry and I have been invited to a party on Saturday."

I said, "That's nice."

I know that Mum likes parties. She is a very sociable sort of person, which is one of the reasons I am such a huge disappointment to her. Mum really loves to be with a crowd! I just sort of shrivel. I am one of those people, if ever I go to a party (which mostly I don't, because no one invites me) who end up standing in the corner with no one to talk to. It makes me feel very self-conscious. Like everyone's looking at me thinking "Look at that boring girl standing in the corner." I know that is what Cindy Williams and Tasha Lansmann would be thinking.

I don't know why it is that I can't behave the same as other people. Sometimes I really wish I could! I am sure it would make my life a whole lot easier, plus it would make Mum happy and stop her worrying over me. I hate it when she worries!

She started worrying this evening, about the party.

"I really don't like leaving you on your own! Couldn't you ask Charlie to come round? Ask her to stay the night!"

I will ask Pilch, as I think it would be quite fun; but as I said to Mum, "I'm fourteen. You don't have to think you can't go places, just because of me."

"I sometimes feel so guilty," said Mum. "I always seem to be out on the razzle!"

I told her that that was all right, she was obviously a razzling kind of person. I said, "It's like having a teenager for a mother."

Mum liked that. She laughed and said, "I still feel

like a teenager!" And then she went all sort of regretful and said, "But it ought to be you going out, not me!"

I immediately thought, Oh, please! Don't start!

She didn't. Not exactly. She just launched into this speech about being a single mum and how difficult it sometimes was, knowing what to do for the best.

"What I desperately don't want," she said, "is to stop you going out and having fun."

"I do have fun," I said.

"Yes, but you know what I mean," said Mum. "I feel you're missing out on so much! And it bothers me that it might be my fault."

I said, "It's not your fault, and I'm not missing out, and in any case we are quite different people."

Mum said, "Yes! I'm just a fun lover. You're far more sensible!"

Even if I hadn't been, she said, there was one thing she had always sworn, right from the beginning, and that was that she would never be an overprotective mother. She looked at me very solemnly as she said this.

"You don't think I'm overprotective, do you? Tell me, Cresta! Tell me if you think I'm overprotective!"

I said, "No, Mum, I don't think you're overprotective."

All the same, it is just as well, I can't help feeling, that I keep my thoughts about Carlito under lock and key... Mum would probably have heart attacks if she knew what my imagination got up to!

Tuesday

Asked Pilch about Saturday. She said she'll have to check with her Mum but she's pretty sure it will be OK. Cindy Williams overheard us and shrieked, "Hey! Wow! What are you two up to?" And then she cackled and said, "Whatever it is, don't do anything I wouldn't!"

I didn't deign to reply, but Pilch can never resist it.

"We're having a sleepover," she said.

"Ooh!" Cindy made her eyes go big. "Just the two of you? Or can anyone join in?"

"I'm afraid we shan't have room for you lot," said Pilch. "We've invited the local football team round."

"Oh, wow!" cried Cindy.

I asked Pilch afterwards why she'd gone and said that about the football team, but she didn't seem to know. It is the silly sort of remark one makes to people such as Cindy. You can't talk sensibly to them.

This evening I was sitting at the dining-room table doing my homework when I suddenly became aware that the room was filled with vapour. I immediately rushed to the door screeching, "Steam! Steam everywhere!"

Mum was on the phone. She put her hand over the mouthpiece and hissed, "Well, turn the kettle off, then!"

I didn't even know the kettle was on. I mean, I was doing my homework! I was writing an essay! I can't be expected to concentrate on two things at once. It was quite uncalled for, what Mum said, about me being wilfully stupid and going round with my head in the clouds thinking I am so superior to everyone else.

I said, "I don't think I'm superior."

"Yes, you do!" said Mum. "You exude it at every pore!"

"At least I'm not a dizzy blonde," I said.

"You can say that again!" said Mum.

She was mad because the bottom of the kettle was burnt out. She went off muttering about yet more expense. Now I suppose I shall have to offer to pay for a new one.

Wednesday

Things are going from bad to worse with me and Mum. Now she says I've broken the vacuum cleaner.

All I was doing was pushing it across my bedroom floor, like you're supposed to do with vacuum cleaners. I mean, that is what vacuum cleaners are for. And the only reason I was doing it in the first place was because Mum said my bedroom looked like a tip. Well! Have I got news for her! If she thinks my bedroom is a tip she should see Pilch's.

I told Mum this. I said, "You're only making me clear up because of Pilch coming to stay the night. You're scared in case she tells her mum we live in a dump. But she wouldn't, because she wouldn't even notice! You could *grow* things in her room."

Mum said she didn't care what you could do in Pilch's room, it was my room she was concerned about. Could I please, she said, just do as she asked and "At least remove a layer of top soil."

So I lugged the vacuum cleaner upstairs and switched it on and pushed it across the floor, and all of a sudden it was like ping! GRAUNCH dong. Total blow out.

I went on to the landing and shrieked, "Mum! The vacuum cleaner's stopped working!"

Mum came pounding up the stairs going, "Now what have you done?"

I said, "I haven't done anything! I only just switched it on."

She could see I'd only just switched it on from the tiny swathe of carpet that was a different colour from the rest.

"You must have caught something in it," fumed Mum.

It is always her first reaction – to blame me when anything happens.

Rather coldly I said, "There wasn't anything to catch. There's obviously something wrong with the thing. Some fundamental flaw."

I mean, if you can't just push a vacuum cleaner across a perfectly flat piece of floor without the thing breaking down, then it has to be faulty workmanship. That's what I would think. Not, "Oh, it must be Cresta's fault." Mum, however, said that it didn't happen when she pushed it across the floor.

"It's you!" she said. "Not bothering to look!"

If that is what they choose to think, there is nothing you can do about it. Teenagers are natural victims.

I sat on my bed and watched sourly as Mum upended the thing and peered at it. I know what she was hoping to find. She was hoping to find an elastic band or a pen top or something, so that she could say "I told you so!" Needless to say there wasn't anything there, so after revving up a few times without any result Mum yanked out the plug and shouted, "First the kettle, now this!"

"Oh, just leave it for Harry," I said. "He'll know what to do."

I couldn't be bothered with it. I just like stuff to work. Washing machines, videos, TV sets. Computers. If they don't, then I get bored. Find someone else to see to them is my motto. I mean, why waste time if you don't have to? But Mum worked herself into a right old froth and bitingly informed me that, "Men aren't here to be our servants, you know! We have to learn to shift for ourselves occasionally."

So we shifted for ourselves and lugged the vacuum cleaner back downstairs and I stood there while Mum took the thing to pieces and nearly electrocuted herself by switching it on and then forgetting to switch it off again while she jabbed inside with a screwdriver, and then she lost one of the screws – which naturally I got blamed for, because she said I was supposed to have been holding them – and finally she took the belt off and couldn't get it back again, so now it has to be left for Harry after all.

And, of course, it is all my fault.

I don't like being on bad terms with Mum, but sometimes it seems I just can't do anything right.

Mum and I have made it up. This is because half way through the night I developed a guilty conscience and decided to humour her and do what she wanted, i.e. clean my bedroom. Just for her. So I dusted all the surfaces with a handkerchief and crawled round the floor on my hands and knees using gobbets of spit to get up all the bits of fluff. I confess I am somewhat amazed at how much has accumulated in three short months. I distinctly remember cleaning my room when Nan came.

Housework is a very trivial occupation. However, it pleased Mum and that is the main thing.

Was going to spend the evening reading *War and Peace* but had a sudden thought about Carlito. He is going to get gored!!! In the bullring!!! He is going to hover 'twixt life and death and be read the last rites (being a Catholic) and everyone will despair. I am going to lie down and think about it. I must get it worked out for Saturday! If Pilch is going to stay over, we can have a good long session.

Friday

In geography today I was happily pursuing my thought about Carlito when I suddenly became aware of two big hairy hands waving in front of my face. Mr Bunting!

"Is anybody the-e-e-ere?" he goes, in this wailing kind of voice.

His breath smells; I think he smokes. I wouldn't want to have an affair with him.

When I got home Mum asked if I would like to go down to the pub with her and Harry.

"It's a lovely evening! We could sit outside, in the garden. Why don't you come?"

She said it in this beseeching sort of voice. I thought that she was probably trying to make up for being mad about the vacuum cleaner (and the kettle) so I said all right I would go, though I didn't specially want to. I just feel that if someone offers you an olive branch it is only gracious to accept it. And I do hate Mum and me being cross with each other.

So I put on a sweater and jeans, thinking this would be good pub-going gear and would meet with Mum's approval, but when I came downstairs her face sort of slithered a few centimetres and she went, "Oh, Cresta! Haven't you got anything better to wear?"

"You mean, like, my mink stole?" I said. Though as a matter of fact I wouldn't be seen dead in a mink stole.

"Couldn't you at least find a different top?" wailed Mum. "Or some jeans that aren't quite so…" She waved a hand. "Unflattering!"

It's what I said: I just can't do anything right. I can't even put the right clothes on. Whatever I'd have put on, it was bound to be wrong. I'm the wrong sort of daughter. I look wrong, I act wrong. I am just one enormous disappointment.

I think some of my feelings must have shown in my face because Mum suddenly hugged me and said, "Darling, I didn't mean to have a go at you! But you can look so much prettier if you try!"

I don't like being a disappointment to Mum. I don't do it on purpose. So I trailed back upstairs and took off the jeans and sweater and put on a shirt and a pair of trousers, and Mum beamed and said, "There! You see? What a difference it makes!" So then I felt happy because she was happy, and Harry was happy because he's always happy, he is just a naturally happy kind of person, and that meant we were all happy, and it is nice when everyone is happy. But then…

Then we got to the pub and the whole evil plot was revealed. Mum is so duplicitous it is just not true!

She lured me there, on purpose. It wasn't because she was trying to make up for being mad. It was because she was trying to pair me off with this boy!

He was sitting there, at the table. My heart just, like, plummeted. I felt like turning round and walking straight out, but I couldn't as I was sandwiched between Mum and Harry. Mum, all bright and burbling, in tones of utter astonishment, goes, "Steven!" Like she was just so surprised to see him there. Like she hadn't known all along.

"Steven! How lovely! This is my daughter, Cresta. Cresta, this is Steven. Jo's son. You know Jo, don't you?"

Jo is one of her loud shrieking friends. She's this woman coming towards us dressed in plastic strips. She's got red hair all piled up like a pineapple, and eyelashes like spokes. She looks about eighteen, but if this boy is her son she can't be. He's at least my age.

He's really geeky. I have to say it. He's got red hair, same as her. He's gelled it, so it's all sticking out in spikes. He's wearing these goofy glasses with lenses the size of cartwheels, and a white T-shirt out of which his scrawny arms and neck protrude like broom handles. Every time he swallows, which is a lot, his Adam's apple bobs up and down like a ping-pong ball. He also has this nervous affliction of cracking his knuckles. His knuckles are huge and knobbly. They go off like gunshots; it's quite alarming. It makes me jump, almost, but nobody else seems to notice. All the rest of them, all Mum and Harry's friends – Jo in her pink plastic strips, and Beth, who has a bum like two ferrets fighting in a bag, and Lisa that sometimes Mum goes line dancing with, and Derek and Darren and Jools, which are the men that belong to them – they're all into their laughing-shrieking routine, leaving me and Steven to get on with it. He's spooky! Like some kind of alien from inner space. He reminds me of a fungus.

It is very wrong to judge people by their looks; I know that. And I try hard not to. But on this occasion I couldn't help it. I was just so angry with Mum! She has no right to deceive me in this way. It was truly embarrassing! We just couldn't find a single thing to talk about. In desperation I asked him if he'd ever read *War and Peace*, and he said no; so then I racked my brains and asked him if he'd read Harry Potter and he said, "You mean that wizard thing?" and I said, "Yes! The wizard thing," thinking this must indeed be some kind of alien if he has to ask who Harry Potter is.

I said, "It's not as rewarding as *War and Peace*" (I am now on page 218) "but it is quite fun." All he said was, "I haven't read it," so that was the end of *that* sparkling bit of conversation.

It wasn't until someone mentioned the word computer that he suddenly sprang into life and started to churn on at great length about chat rooms. He told me how he visits this one particular one that is for hamster enthusiasts. It seems he is really turned on by hamsters! Also by chat rooms. He suggested that perhaps we might visit one together some time. I said, "What, you mean like both using the same computer?" I pictured us cosily sitting side by side. But he said, "No! I could use mine and you could use yours, and then we could meet up and chat."

About what, I ask myself? Hamsters? I told him that in fact we do not have a computer, and his eyes goggled at me behind their saucer-sized lenses. It was like he was now thinking that I must be the one that was some kind of alien. I mean, life without a computer! Wow!

I wonder which is more odd? Not having a computer or not having read Harry Potter? Of course there might be some people that don't have a computer *and* haven't read Harry Potter, though I doubt it. You would practically have to be braindead or live in a cave, I would have thought.

Anyway, from that point on me and Spook sat in this awkward silence, him cracking his knuckles and me gnawing great lumps of flesh out of the side of my thumb, which is now very sore and bleeding, thanks entirely to Mum. Why does she do these things to me???

At least he didn't come back with us afterwards. He mumbled something about having to meet people and went loping off, presumably to indulge in hamster talk with some of his hamster chums. I don't mean to poke fun at hamsters, as I am sure they are very sweet little cuddly things, but I was just so relieved to be rid of him!

Now I have come upstairs to read *War and Peace*, leaving Mum and Harry and their friends downstairs, where from the sound of things they are playing Mum's Dawn of Humanity records. Full blast, as usual. I think I may have to invest in some ear plugs.

Saturday

Harry has just told me that the vacuum cleaner is working again. He said, "I took the sock out."

Triumphantly I turned to Mum and said, "There! I knew Harry would be able to mend it. We could have looked at it all night without realising."

"Realising what, exactly?" said Mum.

I said, "Well, that the sock could be taken out. I mean,

goodness! I wasn't even aware that vacuum cleaners had socks."

"They don't," said Mum. "*This* is the sock." And she held up a mangled-looking object that I recognised (unfortunately) as belonging to me.

"Properly gummed up the works," said Harry. "Beats me how you managed to get it in there."

Mum has said that as a penance I can vacuum the whole of the upstairs for her. In the circumstances I feel it is probably best to just get on and do it.

When I have vacuumed, I am going into town to meet Pilch. We shall probably mooch round the shops and look in Paperback Parade, then we can come back here and read each other our latest episodes, and Pilch will stay the night. I am looking forward to it! It will be fun.

Sunday

Yesterday was a really good day. Lots of things discussed between Pilch and me.

We waited till Mum and Harry had gone off to their party before settling down to read our episodes. Fortunately they left quite early. They were all going to meet up in the pub beforehand. (And get smashed, I bet! Well, that is my reading of the situation.)

I couldn't believe it when I saw what Mum was wearing! She'd got this skirt that was about 20 cm long. *If that.* It was like a sort of… strip.

"Genuine 60s," she burbles. "I paid a fortune for it! What d'you reckon?"

I think my jaw must have clunked open, because Harry, in this smoochy drooly voice, goes, "Doesn't she look a treat? Doesn't she look smashing?"

The thing barely covered her knickers. You could practically see her bum.

I screeched, "Mum! You're not going out like that?"

"Why shouldn't I go out like this?" said Mum, plainly offended.

"Yes, why shouldn't she?" said Harry. And he patted Mum on the aforesaid part of her anatomy, and said that she had a figure to be proud of. "She still looks like a teenager!"

She may look like one. But that doesn't mean she is one! She is my mum, and I felt quite embarrassed for her. I think it is pathetic when older people try to pretend they are still young. It is so belittling!

"Get a load of those legs," said Harry. "Give us a twirl, doll!"

So, guess what? Mum actually starts doing the can-can! Kicking her legs in the air and laughing.

"Whey hey!" cried Harry. "That's my girl!"

Enough said. As they say.

I must confess that I was a bit put out, after Mum and Harry had gone, when instead of commiserating with me, or at any rate maintaining a discreet silence, Pilch giggled and said, "Your mum's a right goer!" Like she thought it was really funny.

"It's since she took up with Harry," I said. "It's made her totally trivial."

"Of course, she's a lot younger than my mum," said Pilch.

"Not that young," I said. "She'll be thirty-three next birthday."

"My mum's forty-eight," said Pilch.

I can't help feeling that in some ways it would be rather a comfort to have a mum that was forty-eight. At least she wouldn't always be making you feel dim and grey and nerdy. It's not appropriate for a mum to go out looking like a teenager and showing her bum! I don't think it is.

I said this to Pilch but she just giggled again and said, "Depends on the bum!"

I thought that was a rather frivolous remark.

We came up to my bedroom to read our episodes. We could have been just as private downstairs, but we always do it in our bedrooms. Bedrooms have the right feel.

Pilch read first. She is into horses now. Not that she has ever been on one, but she has apparently got this book from the library which tells you all about them. She said she felt that Alastair, coming as he does from such an immensely upper class family, would be bound to be what she calls "acquainted with the equestrian arts". So now he is galloping madly back and forth across the Highlands, I beg their pardon, I mean Heelands, on this horse named Monarch of the Glen (ask me not why) that is about two metres tall and "rich sable in colour with a foaming mane and proud arched neck".

Pur-lease!

It wouldn't be so bad if Alastair were the only one that was riding to and fro across the Heelands, but all his friends are riding with him. Pilch describes every single one of their horses in minute detail. She even describes all the tack (horsy term for saddles and bridles and stuff). Plus of course she says what everyone is wearing. Alastair has "cream-coloured jodhpurs and a tweed hacking jacket with a flap".

The flap kills me! I asked her if it was to let the farts out (a fart flap) and she got quite huffy.

Sometimes I find it hard not to giggle when Pilch reads her episodes. But I know that I mustn't, because that would be unkind. It would upset her. I mean, she probably goes to bed and dreams of Alastair in his hacking jacket. With the flap.

Oh, dear! That has set me off again.

After she had read about Alastair on his horse and all his horsy friends, I read my bit about Carlito. About him being gored and hovering 'twixt life and death. I have done a lot more thinking about this. Where he is gored is in the groin, which needless to say is extremely dangerous in more ways than one. His entire manhood could be at stake! For several days, even after he has pulled back from the brink, his fate lies in the balance.

The trouble is, I cannot bring myself to finish the episode. It is like a sort of soap and I am scared that if I finish it I will have nothing to take its place. Not until I can think of something else. Every night in bed I go into "hospital mode" and cannot seem to get out of it.

After we had read our episodes we had this rather intense discussion about sex. It all started because of me saying how Carlito's manhood could be at stake. Pilch said, "You mean, he wouldn't be able to *do* things?" And then she got a bit pink and giggly and said, "Do you think they do?"

I said, "What, you mean Alastair and Carlito?"

I said that as far as I was concerned, Carlito most certainly did! He is what Mum would call a stud. Meaning – he pursues girls like crazy! They also pursue him.

I said this to Pilch. I said, "It is just that I haven't yet got around to thinking of an episode."

Pilch immediately said, "Oh, me too!" She then got even pinker and said, "I wonder what it actually feels like?"

I have often wondered this. It is all very well knowing *how* a thing is done, but that is just the mechanics. Nobody ever thinks to say what it feels like. Which I think is important!

Pilch volunteered the information that she had read somewhere it was like tingling.

"Tingling as in pins and needles?" I said.

Pilch rubbed a finger across her forehead, which is this thing she does when she has embarrassed herself, and said, "Mm... I guess."

I sometimes feel a tingling when I think of Carlito. On the other hand, I have never tingled at the thought of a real live boy. Spooky Steve, for instance. I could look at Spooky Steve all day long and not have one single solitary tingle! More likely I'd just fall asleep through sheer boredom.

I said to Pilch, "We ought to call it the tingle factor."

Pilch said, "Yes. Every time we meet a boy we'll wait to see if they make us tingle!"

It will be interesting…

When we'd finished our discussion about sex we went downstairs and made ourselves some cheese on toast.

"I shouldn't really be eating this," said Pilch. She is a tremendous glutton for cheese.

I asked her why not and she said that her mum had been on at her again about going on a diet. So irresponsible!

After a few moments, pushing her cheese about her plate, Pilch said, "I told Mum the reason I was staying overnight was that we were going to a party."

I gaped at her. "What on earth did you say that for?"

Pilch mumbled, "Janine's going to one."

"So what?" I said.

Pilch just humped a shoulder and messed a bit more with her cheese.

"Would you want to go to parties?" I said.

"Not specially," said Pilch. "Not unless—"

I said, "Unless what?"

"Well! I mean." She giggled. "I'd go if it was Alastair!"

"Perhaps you ought to make him have one," I said. "Then you could choose what you were going to wear to it."

"Yes, and I wouldn't be fat," said Pilch.

It is going to be too utterly boring if Pilch starts to fuss about the way she looks.

After our cheese on toast we sat up watching videos until Mum and Harry came back. We watched one that was complete rubbish called *Spawn of the Bloodsucking Vampires*, which even though it was rubbish was quite spine-chilling in a mindless kind of way. And then, as an antidote, we watched *Thelma & Louise*, which is one of my big faves. It is one of Mum's too.

Mum and I used to watch a lot of movies. We used to go to the video store every Saturday and take out two videos and sit there all evening with packets of crisps and bottles of Coke (or sometimes wine, in Mum's case).

I used to enjoy our Saturday evenings. We got to be real movie buffs! We hardly ever do it any more; only just occasionally if for some reason Harry's on an evening shift, which he hardly ever is since he also enjoys his Saturday evenings with Mum. They usually go off razzling somewhere. Clubbing. Pubbing. Partying. This of course is what happens when a man comes into your life. Big sigh! Though I do try very hard not to begrudge her.

Now I have distracted myself and can't remember where I was. I know! Pilch and me were watching *Thelma & Louise*. We had just reached the bit at the end, where they are about to drive over the edge of the Grand Canyon, when Mum and Harry arrived back. (I didn't mind missing that bit as a) I know it off by heart and b) it always makes my stomach churn.) Mum was rather loud and giggly, which means she had been drinking. I think Harry had, too, as his face was all red, but it was OK as they took a cab. Harry is dead against drink-driving, I suppose because he drives for a living.

On the whole I will say for him that he has a great many good points, the main one being that he makes Mum happy, but also of course he comes in handy for such manly tasks as removing socks from vacuum cleaners. I guess I wouldn't mind too much if he and Mum were to get married. I am growing used to the thought of his bum on the lavatory seat and his underpants in the washing.

This morning, unfortunately, Pilch had to go home as her auntie and uncle are coming. She said she did not specially want to see her auntie and uncle as she had seen them only a few weeks ago, but her mum had said that she had to be there. She said this was because her cousin Andy will be with them. He is fifteen and Pilch's mum is always scheming for him and Pilch to do things together.

"Like, why don't we go to Thorpe Park? Why don't we meet up in town? Why don't we go to a movie?"

Just like Mum and Spooky Steve!

I'm feeling a bit flat now that I'm on my own. I can't seem to settle to anything. I tried having some more thoughts about Carlito, but nothing came. No tingle! Next I tried reading some more of *War and Peace*, but either I have reached a particularly draggy patch or I am just not in the mood. So then I went and stared out of the window at the boringly familiar Sunday scene of people washing their cars. Awesome! Nothing ever happens in the suburbs on a Sunday. The most exciting thing is going to Ikea, which is what Mum and Harry have done.

While I was glooming out of the window I saw Tasha Lansmann walking down the road with Brad Sullivan. They were holding hands. I wonder if he makes her tingle???

Monday

(4th Week)

Asked Pilch how it went with her cousin. She said, "It was all right, but there wasn't any tingle factor."

Mum, meanwhile, is still going on about Spooky Steve. I might have known she wouldn't let it drop.

"He's such a nice boy," she said. "Don't you think?"

I agreed that he was, because I think probably any boy that loves his hamsters has got to be pretty nice.

Mum was obviously pleased with this reply. She got all encouraged by it.

"So have you arranged to see each other again?" she chirps, trying (without success, I may say) to sound casual.

I said no, we hadn't. "He wanted us to meet in a chat room and I had to tell him, we don't have a computer."

"Oh! Oh, Cresta!" Mum looked at me, stricken. No computer! Oh, tragedy! How can I meet boys if we don't have a computer?

"We ought to get you one," she said.

Well, we ought, I agree; but not for that reason.

"We will!" said Mum. "We'll get one! Tell him we're getting one!"

"Mum, it's all right, you don't have to panic," I said. "I didn't want to meet him, anyway."

"Why not?" said Mum. "Meet in a chat room! It sounds like fun!"

"It might be," I said, "if we had anything to chat about."

"You'd find something!"

"I don't think so," I said. "He's into hamsters. Hamsters is really all he can talk about."

"Oh, don't be so silly!" said Mum. "And don't be so unkind! The poor boy is probably just shy."

"Well, maybe I'm shy, too," I said.

"You're not shy," said Mum. "You just have this huge superiority complex!" She was starting to sound distinctly annoyed. I'd obviously gone and upset her again. "What right have you to sneer at Steven for liking hamsters?"

I explained that I was not sneering. I told her that I would far rather have a boy that loved hamsters than a boy that loved for instance football. I don't feel that I could ever get into football, whereas hamsters are no doubt quite endearing creatures.

"I just don't want to go and chat about them!"

Mum simply refuses to see my point of view. She said that I was most ungracious and that there was no pleasing me.

It is extremely unfair of her to say this. I was pleased on Saturday, when Pilch came. I am pleased when I am having thoughts about Carlito. I am pleased when I am reading *War and Peace*. (Usually.) I am pleased about lots of things. They just don't happen to be the things that Mum would like me to be pleased about. That is all.

Tuesday

For dinner today Pilch said she was going to eat "just vegetables and fruit". She then went and helped herself to a handful of French fries off my plate! I could have stopped her but I didn't as I feel she should be encouraged to go on eating normally rather than starving herself of proper nutrients. I don't fancy the idea of my best friend going into a decline!

Pilch moaned, "This is awful! I have no self-control at all!"

Cindy Williams, who was sitting at our table, had to go and shove her oar in. She said, "If you carry on like that you won't have any waistline, either!" She said it just as Pilch was in the act of swallowing a chip. Poor old Pilch nearly choked.

I said, "Waistlines are hardly of much importance in the overall scheme of things, I wouldn't have thought."

"What would you know about it?" said Cindy, with this sort of sneer on her lips.

Thinking no doubt that she was coming to my rescue, not that I needed it – I take absolutely no notice whatsoever of Cindy Williams and her trivial mouthings – Pilch spluttered, "She's a lot thinner than you are!"

Cindy said, "Yeah, she'll go out with the bath water if she's not careful! Call that a figure? More like a piece of string!"

When I got home I said to Mum, "Pilch's mum is trying to push her into anorexia! She wants her to go on a diet."

There are times when Mum can be really disappointing. Instead of agreeing with me that this was an appalling way for any self-respecting mother to behave, she said that Pilch could certainly do with "losing a bit".

I said, "Mu-um!" in reproachful tones. "She's not fat!"

"No, but she'd look better if she slimmed down," said Mum. "She could be quite attractive if she got rid of a few kilos."

I am truly ashamed of Mum for being so trivial.

Have just examined myself in the mirror. Have a huge redness appearing on my chin. I think it is going to be a spot.

Wednesday

This morning Mrs Adey gave us our essays back. The ones we did last week. I am totally knocked out! She has given me an A*!!! At the bottom she has written, "An excellent piece of work! Extremely well thought out."

I knew it was good when I wrote it. But I didn't know it was that good! What it's about is reading the classics.

I say how you have to persevere. How they may not seem like a whole lot of fun while you're reading them, but when you reach the end you realise how rewarding they have been. I thought that Mrs Adey would approve of this. But at the same time it is what I truly believe! In a moment I am going to get to grips with *War and Peace* again.

I told Mum about my A*. She cried, "Oh, Cresta, that's wonderful! What a clever daughter I've got!" And then she narrowed her eyes in the direction of my chin and said, "Have you been picking that spot?"

I immediately said no, though in fact I had. Mum, in vexed tones, said, "I do wish you wouldn't! You'll make such a mess of yourself."

This annoyed me quite considerably. I retorted, "So what?"

Mum said, "So you really ought to start learning to take a bit more pride in your appearance is what!"

Sullenly – I didn't mean to be sullen, but she gets me so mad! – I said, "Why? And for whose benefit?"

"Yours!" snapped Mum. "And don't look at me like that! You'll thank me when you're a bit older."

"Doubt it," I said.

I expect that was a rather silly sort of remark, and probably rude, as well, but it seems Mum and me simply cannot help but rub each other up the wrong way. Rather than going on about spots, for instance, why couldn't she have asked me what my essay was about?

"Tell me about your essay, Cresta! Let us discuss it together."

But oh, no! Just, don't make a mess of yourself. Because if you do, NO BOY WILL LOOK AT YOU.

Trivial, trivial, trivial!

I have just squeezed the head out of my spot and now there is a great gaping hole. It is like peering into the depths of a volcano. During the night it will probably gather up its forces, ready to erupt, in a great swoosh of horrible yellow pus. How disgusting are bodily functions!

Thursday

Chin looks like a bomb crater. Mum pursed her lips but didn't actually say anything. Just as well, since I wasn't in the mood for it.

When I got to school Pilch went, "Ooooh! You've made a right mess of yourself!"

Felt like hitting her.

Coming home on the bus I saw a boy on the building site at the corner of Delamere Road who looked just like Carlito!

Friday

Pilch back to eating macaroni cheese. Hooray! I knew she wouldn't be able to keep to a diet for very long.

Got off the bus two stops early on the way home so I could walk past Delamere Road and see if the Carlito boy was there. He was! He has this very glossy black hair, just like Carlito, and was stripped to the waist and a beautiful brown colour even though it is October. This could either mean a) that he has just come back from holiday or b) that he is naturally that colour. I think it is more likely to be the latter. I think he is probably Spanish!

As I walked past, pretending not to look but sort of squinching up from under my lashes, he came towards me wheeling a barrow. I felt myself grow very hot and red and wished after all that I had not picked my spot.

Was going to read some more of *War and Peace* but think I shall lie down and have some tingly thoughts, instead.

Met Pilch in the shopping centre and went on a search for a birthday present for Mum. Not that I think, at this moment in time, that she really deserves one, but it is always possible that by the time her birthday comes round she will have redeemed herself by a) taking a bit more interest in my achievements, b) not nagging about my lack of a social life and c) not trying to fix me up with every stray boy that comes her way. Then, if I had not got her one, I would feel mean. So I said to Pilch, "Better to be safe than sorry, as they say."

Pilch said, "What are you going to get her? What do you think she would like?"

I said, "Clothes, probably." But Mum's taste in clothes and mine are very different. I wouldn't know what to buy her. Pilch suggested make-up or a bottle of perfume, but again I wouldn't know what to buy.

We went all round the shops without finding a single thing. The sort of stuff I thought she might like, such as Wedgewood pots and glass vases, was all way too expensive. Pilch, trying to be helpful, kept pouncing on little dinky donkeys wearing straw hats, or plastic owls with holes in their heads for stashing pens; or even, if you can believe it, miniature garden gnomes (for window boxes, I presume). The garden gnomes particularly entranced her. There were fishing gnomes and smoking gnomes and cogitating gnomes. There was even a squatting gnome, which looked somewhat vulgar to me. Pilch went into raptures.

"Look!" she squealed. "Gnomes!"

I said, "I am not getting Mum a gnome."

"But they're so sweet," crooned Pilch.

"They're hideous," I said. The sort of thing I would

have bought when I was too young to know better. I do try to be a little bit cultured.

Pilch fell into a tremendous sulk when I wouldn't buy Mum a gnome.

"Buy one for your mum," I said.

"Not her birthday," said Pilch.

I said, "Well, then, buy one for yourself! If you want one that much. I think they're grotesque."

"I know they are," said Pilch. "That's what makes them so cute!"

I have made a mental note to buy her one for Christmas. In the meantime, there is still the problem of Mum. I shall have to do some thinking about it. I shall see if she redeems herself!

On our way to Paperback Parade, partly to look at the books but mainly, I must confess, to have a cup of heavenly gorgeous hot chocolate (they float marshmallows on the top. It is so yummy!) we passed Cindy and Tasha. Tasha was with Brad Sullivan, Cindy with some other boy. Tasha looked like she and Brad Sullivan had been bonded together with some kind of cement.

As soon as we were safely, I most sincerely hope, out of earshot, Pilch, with a simpery sort of sigh, said "I wouldn't mind so much if they looked like him."

I said, "If who looked like him?"

"All the drongoidal geeks our mums keep trying to palm off on us," said Pilch. "All we get is Andy Pandy and Spooky Steve." I'd told her about him, heedless to say. "I wouldn't mind being palmed off with someone like Brad Sullivan!"

I reminded her that my mum *had* tried to palm me off with Brad Sullivan.

"And you didn't want him!" squeaked Pilch.

I narrowed my eyes and said, "He doesn't make you tingle, does he?"

"We-e-ell…" Pilch gave this little squiggle. (A cross between a wriggle and a squirm.) "He does sort of."

"*Brad Sullivan?*" I said.

"He's kind of cute," said Pilch. And then she giggled and said, "I think it's his bum!"

There are times when I do grow seriously worried about Pilch. It's happening more and more! First parties, now Brad Sullivan. Surely she can't really fancy him? Where is this all going to lead???

I don't think I could bear it if me and Pilch grew apart. We have known each other so long, we have done so many things together! We have had such fun! There was our secret language that we used, and our puppet theatre that we made, and our musical that we wrote. I can still remember our musical! Jack and the Beanstalk.

"Jack-have-you-washed-behind-your-ears?" all on one note.

Not very inspired! But we were only nine. And then there was our play that we did – "For two people in ten-and-a-half acts". We thought ten-and-a-half acts was so cool! And the magazine we wrote, that everybody had to buy a copy of. My mum, and Pilch's mum, and our nans, and Pilch's auntie, and our next-door neighbours. And the school photo that we made, all across my bedroom wall, when we collected faces out of magazines and newspapers and stuck them up and put names underneath them. Funny names! And grotesque faces. One of them was a pig. We called it Pansy Porker after a girl in our class that we didn't like. I'd probably call it Cindy Williams if I did it now. Although, upon reflection, why insult pigs?

I don't mean to be morbid, but I really would hate it if one of us fell by the wayside. It wouldn't be the same if I got to uni and Pilch didn't!

I blame her mum. All that nagging at her, to go on a diet. It has obviously made her feel insecure.

This morning Mum and Harry went buzzing off to yet another record fair. Still in search of the elusive album! I said, "Honestly, is it really worth it?"

Harry rather fiercely said that "Anything your mum wants is worth it!"

He must be really besotted. It is rather touching, in its way. He is so big and beefy looking! You wouldn't think he had this softer side to him. He is quite a nice bloke, really.

"You don't think," I said, "that you are on a wild-goose chase?"

"What does it matter if we are?" said Mum, gaily. "It's fun just going to the fairs!"

She gets all dressed up for them. Today she was wearing tight-as-tight jeans, cowboy boots and an old leather biker jacket that she bought years ago when I was in juniors and she was going with this guy that had a Harley Davidson. Harry has a black cab! He dropped me off at school in it the other morning and Cindy Williams saw me. I didn't tell her that Harry was my mum's boyfriend. I pretended that I had just, like, suddenly, on a whim, decided to come to school by taxi!

Anyway, I wished Mum good luck, because it seems she really really does want this album (search for lost youth, etc.) and then I came up here to just generally potter and have thoughts and maybe do a bit of reading. While I was pottering the phone rang, so I went down to answer it and it was Nan.

"Dee?" she said. "Is that you?"

I said, "No, it's Cresta. Mum's out."

Nan said, "Oh. Gone with that Harry, I suppose?"

Nan doesn't approve of Harry. She thinks he is

coarse. I guess he is, in a way – I mean, some of the expressions he comes out with! – but he obviously loves Mum to bits and as far as I am concerned that is the only thing that matters. I know that I go on about Mum rather a lot, and it is true she can make me truly mad, but I do very much want her to find happiness.

I said to Nan that she and Harry had gone to a record fair and probably wouldn't be back until tea time. She said, "That's all right! That means you and I can have a little chat."

I was a bit alarmed by this, as you never quite know, with Nan, what she is going to chat about, like sometimes she has this tendency to lecture and I can't stand that. Last time she rang it was manners she wanted to lecture about, i.e. how young people don't have any. Which was pretty much of a cheek considering that whenever she stays I make a point of rushing frantically about, opening doors and pulling out chairs and fetching her glasses, which she is for ever leaving in totally inappropriate places such as inside the airing cupboard or on top of the loo.

"We never get a chance to talk," she said.

She wanted to know how I was getting on, so I told her about school, and about Mrs Adey giving me an A* for my essay, and Nan made this little cooing noise and

said, "Well! Imagine that! We have a genius in the family."
After which there was a bit of a pause, and then, all coy
and mock sort of casual, she goes, "And how about
boyfriends? I'll bet you've got a whole string of them!"

Why is it I have this strong suspicion that Mum has
been talking to her???

I said, "I don't really have time for boys right now.
I'm too busy with school work."

"Very sensible," said Nan. "Don't feel you have to
apologise for it."

When Nan said that it made me feel like I was some
kind of freak. Maybe she thinks I'm a lesbian, too.

"Now, look, pet," she said, "don't you worry about it!
I know your mum frets herself, thinks you don't get out
enough. But just because she was a tearaway doesn't
mean that you have to be. I never could get that girl to
settle to her studies! I tried everything I knew. But she
wouldn't have it. She was all over the place! You're
different. You mustn't let her push you into things
before you're ready for it. You'll come to it in your
own good time. You're just a bit of a slow developer,
that's all. And none the worse for it, in my opinion!"

This is all very well, but I am not sure how much I
value Nan's opinion. I'm glad she accepts that I am
different. And I'm glad she thinks that it's wrong of

Mum to try and push me. But what does she mean, I am a slow developer???

Afterwards I came upstairs and brooded about it. I can't understand why Mum keeps hassling me all the time! I mean, considering her own love life has been one total and utter disaster. Ever since I can remember, Mum has been let down by men. These are just a few of the ones I can bring to mind:

Mick, the biker with the Harley Davidson. The bike was great, but Mick was a real slimeball. He used to disappear for weeks on end and never let her know where he was or if he was coming back. One time, I remember, she prepared this big spread for his birthday and he never even turned up. Poor Mum! She just put her head on the table and cried and cried.

Then there was Gerry. He was another one that made her cry. She really thought they were an item, her and Gerry, till it turned out he'd been two-timing her all along. Only had a wife and three kids back home in Ireland, didn't he?

And Paul, the con man. Took her for a right ride. And Robbie, who did drugs. Robbie was seriously bad news. Then there was Tariq, the fun-loving movie star. *Said* he was a movie star, back home in India. OK, so he looked dead gorgeous, but boy was he a creep! What right did he have to make Mum feel she was inferior? He got her so wound up she hardly dared open her mouth. But there you go! If she will fall for these airheads.

And I haven't yet mentioned Joss. Joss was the pits! He was the worst. He was pond life. Just strung her along till something better turned up, then ditched her. "Sorry, doll! You know how it is. And anyway, you're old!"

It took Mum ages to get over that. I honestly thought she never would. That was when we started renting movies every Saturday and became big movie buffs. Then Harry came into her life, and he's the first guy that's ever treated her right. Of course, he doesn't look much. Shortish, darkish, a bit what I would call squat. And he's not exactly exciting. I didn't think it would last five minutes, but it has. In some ways it's almost like having a read dad about the place. The others weren't dads. They were like total twonks.

All I'm saying, you'd think Mum would be glad I'm not following in her footsteps. That's all.

Monday

(5th Week)

I know what I am going to buy Mum for her birthday. I am going to buy her a record! Or maybe even two records, if they don't cost too much. Old ones, natch! Something from when she was young.

There is this second-hand record store in town called Dandy's. It was Pilch who told me about it. She said, "They have millions of records! You might be able to find one for your mum."

It would be brilliant if I could find something by her favourite band. I might even be able to find THE ALBUM! I have decided that Mum deserves it, in spite of talking to Nan about me behind my back and trying to pair me off with Spooky Steve.

My change of heart is because she came back from the record fair last night with a prezzie for me: a video of my all-time ace favourite movie, which is called *Dog Day Afternoon* with Al Pacino. It is somewhat prehistoric, though not as prehistoric as *Some Like it Hot*, which is one that Mum and Harry swoon over.

It is all about how Al Pacino tries to rob a bank to pay for his lover (another man!) to have a sex-change operation. I am aware that this sounds distinctly dubious, not to say totally wacky, but it is both funny and touching and ultimately sad, as it all ends in disaster. Al Pacino is arrested, his lover isn't in the least bit grateful (he is rather a neurotic wreck, to tell the truth), and a poor friend that he has talked into robbing the bank with him, and who is rather simple and keeps saying in a pathetic way that he cannot face going back to prison, well he is shot and killed, which always makes me shed tears.

There are those people, I suppose, who would say

that he deserves to be shot for robbing a bank, but I do not look at it that way.

Mum says she cannot for the life of her see what I like so much about this curious movie. I am not very sure myself as a matter of fact, but it is based on a true story and I have seen it twice, once on television and once when Mum rented it from the video store. Now I can watch it whenever I want!

Pilch, who has also seen it, says that it is OK. "But nothing special." I beg to differ! She says the reason it gets to me is because Al Pacino reminds me of Carlito. She says that is why I chose the name Carlito because Al Pacino has done another film called *Carlito's Way*. (Which I have also seen, and which also makes me cry.)

Unfortunately, alas, Al Pacino is now quite old and doesn't look in the least like Carlito! But maybe when he was young he did; just a little bit. It is so sad when people get old! Like Brigitte Bardot who I once saw a picture of when she was young and pretty, and now when you see her she is this very wrinkled aged person like a grandmother. Perhaps after all it is better to die young, like Marilyn Monroe or James Dean (who Mum says was an icon) then that is how you will always be remembered.

But to get back to Mum! She was really happy that

she had found my movie for me.

"Look," she cried, "look what I've got! I saw it there, and I thought, Cresta would love this! It's only second-hand, of course."

I wouldn't care if it was third-hand! I will treasure it for always. It was so sweet of Mum to buy it!

As well as my Al Pacino movie, Mum also bought a video of Queen, that is another band she really likes. We all sat down to watch it, with Mum and me (but not Harry!) sighing over poor Freddie Mercury, who tragically died of AIDS. He was very charismatic and I lay awake half the night having morbid thoughts about Carlito, which became more and more morbid as the night wore on. I am very suggestible like that. The least little thing, and if it appeals to the imaginative/creative/romantic side of me I immediately spin whole sagas out of it. By morning I had almost an entire new episode worked out!

Looked for the Carlito boy on the building site on the way home from school, but he wasn't there. I hope it doesn't mean he's disappeared for good!

Tuesday

Walked round the playing field with Pilch at lunch time and told her my morbid thoughts about Carlito. She did not share my enthusiasm.

"Well, he's your character," she said. "But just remember, once he's gone, he's gone."

It is one of our unspoken rules. Once a thought has been solidified, i.e. written down, there is no turning back. You can't, like, resurrect anyone. That would be cheating. It would take away any semblance of reality.

I said to Pilch that I hadn't thought so much of Carlito actually dying (not for quite some time, anyhow) but more of being sick and nobly suffering.

"Like Chopin," I said, "dying of consumption." We did Chopin with Mrs Bromley last term. I can't say I much like his music, but dying of consumption is always tragic.

"Chopin was ugly," said Pilch, in an irrelevant kind of way. "Most of them were. All those old composer people. Like Schubert. He was dead ugly. He died of syphilis," she added.

I said, "Really?" We then got a bit sidetracked, talking about syphilis and about poor Schubert being so ugly. I asked Pilch how she knew about it, and she said she'd read it in a book called Condensed Composers. Pilch does read some very odd things! But I suppose it is all knowledge.

We didn't get back to Carlito until it was time for afternoon school.

"I just don't see how you can do this to him!" hissed Pilch.

I agree it is weird that one can have these kind of thoughts about one's characters. Why do I think of it as romantic? I know it isn't, really. I know there's nothing in the least romantic about being sick. It's the thought of someone young and beautiful being sick. That's why it is so sad about poor Schubert and Chopin. They were young, but they were not beautiful, and so it's not romantic.

This is an exceedingly shallow way to think, but it cannot be helped. It is the truth.

Still having morbid thoughts. They are getting morbider and morbider! Have been lying under the duvet, daydreaming, instead of doing my homework. (Which is only geography, so doesn't really matter.)

Have just made a discovery: if I clasp my hands behind my back and squeeze I can make my elbows touch. I wonder if this is something that anyone can do or if it's just me???

Carlito boy back on building site! Browner than ever. I definitely felt the Tingle Factor…

Thursday

The most embarrassing day of my entire life! Went into town with Mum to do some late-night shopping. She wanted to get a hat to wear for some wedding that she and Harry have been invited to. I still can't really understand what she wanted me to be there for. To advise her, she said.

"Stop me buying something foolish and unsuitable!"

Which is plainly ridiculous, since she never listens to a word I say.

"Mum!" goes my frequent anguished cry. "You're not going out dressed like that?"

"Why not?" she ripostes. (A word I have just learnt.) "What's wrong with it?"

You can't really tell your own mum that she's wearing clothes that are way too young for her. She just thinks I don't have any dress sense. So why ask me to go and choose hats?

Well, anyway. It wasn't the hat that was the problem. All hats are pretty stupid, if you ask me. The one Mum chose wasn't any stupider than any of the others. A sort of blue cartwheel affair with feathery bits. The embarrassing part came afterwards when she suddenly spied some jeans going cheap and decided that she had to have a pair.

"I mean, look, Cresta! Twenty-five per cent off! That's a bargain!"

She'd have liked me to have some, too, but they were men's ones and were all too big.

"You're so beautifully slim," sighed Mum.

I told her that she was quite slim, too, which pleased her. It is not more than the truth but unfortunately it was the wrong thing to say as it gave her the idea she might be small enough to fit into a size 28, so off she trolled into a cubicle with some 28 regulars over her arm while I hung about outside and scanned the horizon for any Carlito types. Not a single one!

After a bit it occurred to me that Mum was taking an inordinately long time, just trying on a pair of humble jeans, I mean there's not much to it. Well, not if you do it in the normal way that everyone else would do it. Like just taking your shoes and your skirt off and sticking your legs into the leg holes. Dead easy!

But oh, no! That wasn't the way that Mum had done it. I knew there was something wrong when I stepped into the changing room area and heard these thumpings and bangings coming from one of the cubicles.

"Mum?" I said.

I peered round the curtain to see Mum rolling about the floor on her back, like an upended turtle, performing prodigies of contortion with her legs in the air.

"What are you doing?" I said.

"I am trying," panted Mum, "to get – out – of these – jeans!"

In her eagerness to get into them, and prove that she was a size 28, she had actually pulled them on over her boots, her cowboy boots. Now, lo and behold, they wouldn't come off!

"They're narrow leg," giggled Mum, as she wriggled and squirmed. I don't know what she found so funny about it! Her face was bright scarlet. "Do something!" she said.

"Like what?" I said. "What am I supposed to do? Why didn't you take the boots off first?"

"Oh, shut up!" said Mum.

She had pulled the jeans down as far as they would go and was doing her best to peel them off inside out. Naturally, they wouldn't come. They wouldn't go over the heels of the boots.

"Look, just stop thrashing about," I said. I was nervous someone was going to come and investigate. I mean, they must have thought a murder was going on, the racket Mum was making.

I grabbed hold of one of her legs and started tugging at the boot that was at the end of it. Needless to say, the boot wouldn't come, either. The boot was caught in the jean and the jean was caught in the boot. Impasse!

"What are we going to do?" giggled Mum.

I said, "Maybe you should just pull them back up and say you want to wear them now."

"I can't," giggled Mum. Totally unabashed. "They're too tight! They won't zip!"

She was right: they wouldn't. I got her to stand up

and used every ounce of strength to at least tug the wo sides together, but they wouldn't even meet across her stomach.

I said, "Try pulling your sweater down! Maybe it won't show."

But the sweater wasn't long enough. So then I thought of buying a coat that she could put over the top, but Mum said she didn't need a coat, she couldn't afford a coat. And anyway, she said, she didn't trust me to go and choose one for her.

"We'll just have to get the boots off," she said. "Either that, or call the fire brigade!"

So down she went again, bang, plummet! on to her back, and there was me, hauling and tugging and bright scarlet just like Mum, with great globules of sweat dripping off me, and all of a sudden, without any warning, a boot comes shooting off with such force it propels me right out of the cubicle, across the gangway and into the one opposite, where some poor woman, half naked, is trying on a dress. It was just so embarrassing.

A few minutes ago Harry rang up and I heard Mum telling him all about what had happened, like it was the funniest thing since Charlie Chaplin in silent movies. Which actually I don't find very funny at all, to tell the truth.

"Cresta's ashamed of me," gurgled Mum. "But oh, dear! You would have laughed!"

To think that Mum is going to be thirty-three next birthday. And she is still behaving like a child!

Friday

Still can't bear to think of yesterday. No one can say I don't have a sense of humour, I laugh uproariously at certain things. I fail, however, to see anything in the least bit amusing in Mum rolling about on her back making grunting noises with a pair of jeans round her ankles. That is just shame-making.

She and Harry have gone to meet their friend at the

pub. I bet she's telling them all about it. She is a terrible exhibitionist! And Harry just makes her worse. He encourages her. I can't imagine why she should be like this, when I am not and neither is Nan. Nan likes to think of herself as "refined". She would be horrified if she knew half the things Mum gets up to!

I am pretty horrified myself. But I, alas, have to live with it.

Now I am going to resolutely turn my mind away from Mum and her antics and write down my latest thoughts for tomorrow, for reading to Pilch. I am going to take the plunge! Carlito is going to die young... a slow, romantic death (like poor Leonardo in *Titanic*). Not in this particular episode, I hasten to add. This is just the beginning. I can make it last for as long as I want! Months, or even years. Today is when the doctors break the news. I dreamt it up in bed last night!

Oh, heavens! Mum and Harry are back and they have brought people with them. I can hear them all laughing and talking. Now I suppose they will start making noise.

Yes! There they go. Screech honk hoot. I bet they've all drunk too much!

Mum has just looked round my bedroom door and said, "Cresta! I've been telling everyone how stupid I was yesterday. Why don't you come down and help me act it out?"

No, thank you! Once was quite enough.

Went into Dandy's with Pilch to see if we could find Mum's record. It is huge! It has four floors, of which number four is where you can buy food and drink and memorabilia, such as postcards, posters, books, etc. The other three are all divided up into different sorts of music, e.g. pop, soul, jazz, punk, rock and so on, and then into years. We didn't know where to start looking!

"When in doubt, ask," said Pilch, and without more ado she went scooting across to where two boys, wearing green sweats with DANDY'S written on the front, were sticking price labels on to records.

"Excuse me," she goes, in this very loud penetrating voice that half the shop can hear. "'Scuse me! We're looking for an album by this group called Dawn of Humanity?"

I was about to hastily explain that it wasn't for ourselves – we weren't the ones who wanted this grungy old music – when one of the boys goes, "In that case, you have come to the right hombre!"

Hombre. That's Spanish!

He asked which album it was that we were after, and before I could even open my mouth Pilch goes, "Driftwood?"

Like it was her mum we were buying it for! This begins to seriously annoy me, I mean Pilch just taking over, especially as this boy is speaking Spanish. I mean, what's it to do with her? She can be really pushy at times. So I elbowed her out of the way and said how it was for my mum, for her birthday.

"Imagine! It came out when she was 16!" gushed Pilch.

"1985," I said, glaring rather hard at her.

The boy said, "Hombre! That is a long time ago."

I don't think he can actually be Spanish as his name is Sean, which sounds more Irish. But it is rather a coincidence, I cannot help feeling. Especially as it was me he smiled at, not Pilch, in spite of her having been so pushy and done most of the talking.

He said, "Let's go take a look," and led us upstairs to this section marked ROCK. The other boy (whose name is Tom. Very ordinary!) came with us, I am not sure why as we could have looked quite well by ourselves, but he engaged Pilch in conversation and that was good as it meant me and Sean could concentrate on the job in hand, i.e. finding Mum's album. Except that we couldn't as it wasn't there. Apparently, it is very sought after.

Sean said, "How about this one? Does she have this one?" showing me a bright purple record sleeve with the word GLADIATOR spilling across it in what looked like blood.

I said, "I don't think so. I don't remember seeing it." Which I surely would have done!

Sean said that if Mum was a fan then GLADIATOR was a must-have.

"It's a classic!"

I inquired rather nervously how much it was, as I had

seen several records marked as high as £25. Twenty-five pounds for a record!!! (But I have since learnt that some people pay hundreds.)

Sean said, "Call it a tenner. How about that?"

He had his thumb over the price as he said it, and when we went back downstairs he took out his little zapping machine and zapped another label on it saying £10, so that I am almost certain he knocked some off for me. I can't think why! Pilch, later on, rather meanly suggested that he may in fact have added some.

"He could see you were a soft touch!"

I think she was just miffed because of Sean obviously preferring me to her.

Before we left I asked if the album was ever likely to come in. Because, I mean, if it did, I could always buy it for Mum's Christmas present. Sean promised that he would keep an eye open for it. He said, "It does turn up from time to time."

He then said why didn't I leave my address and telephone number so that he could let me know? Whereupon Pilch instantly jumped in and said, "I'll give you mine, as well!"

Why did she think he would want hers??? I asked her this when we had left the shop, and she looked a bit flustered, so that I could tell she was desperately trying to think of some rational-sounding excuse. In the end all she could come up with was, "Um, well, you know! In case you might be out, or something."

Pathetic!

Sean said that he and Tom are there every Saturday, and will also be there over half term. He said, "You could always drop by and check what's come in. We have new stuff all the time." He said there are other albums by the same group that Mum might like. So I expect that is what we shall do. (I say we as we are used to doing things together and also it would be a bit mean if I were to sneak in there without Pilch. Though no more than she deserves. I mean, pushing herself forward like that!)

After leaving Dandy's we did a bit of shopping then went back to Pilch's place and tried out Mum's album on Pilch's mum and dad's old record player. Her mum came in while it was playing and said, "My goodness! That takes me back a bit!"

Pilch said, "It's for her mum. She wants to be young again."

"It's her new boyfriend," I said. "She's gone all girly."

Pilch's mum said, "Good for her! I'd go all girly if I had a new boyfriend."

"Would you like one?" said Pilch.

Pilch's mum laughed and said, "At my age? I should be so lucky!"

But we both knew she was only joking; she wouldn't really want one. Pilch's mum and dad think the world of each other. Pilch says they are a real fuddy duddy old married couple. Maybe Mum and Harry will end up like that. I wouldn't mind! But I cannot seriously imagine it. Mum is just so dizzy!

After we'd listened to the album we went up to Pilch's room to read our latest episodes. Pilch's was quite adventurous! For her. All about Alastair "lying in the heather" with a girl called Zara, who is "just sixteen and very curvaceous." Pilch isn't sixteen, but she is curvaceous. I couldn't help wondering…

"Do they do it?" I said.

Pilch turned scarlet and said, "Yes, but I can't read it out."

She wouldn't, no matter how hard I pushed. I said reproachfully that we had never before kept things private, but I could see that it was embarrassing her. I said, "Is it a Passionate Love scene?"

"Sort of," said Pilch. But she still wouldn't read it! She said maybe sometime I could read it for myself. But not today!

"Anyway, it's your turn," she said. She was all of a

ferment to hear about Carlito and whether I had done what she calls The Dreadful Deed.

At this point I have a confession to make. For the first time in my life I have told Pilch a lie. I mean, a real whopping big one. I told her that I hadn't written anything down...

I don't know what brought it on, but quite suddenly I started having these tremendous second thoughts. I don't want Carlito to grow pale and thin! I don't want him to die! I must have been mad ever to think of it! It is sick. Sick sick sick. And I am a sick person! I have a diseased imagination.

So now I have torn up all the pages that I wrote, about the doctor breaking the news, and I have burnt them. I set fire to them in my waste paper basket, and Mum yelled up the stairs, "Cresta, what are you doing? You'll burn the house down!"

I told Pilch that I had changed my mind. I said, "I toyed with the idea, but it was kind of a dead end." Which ho ho ho would be a joke if it weren't so sick.

I could see that one part of Pilch was a bit disappointed, as I think secretly, whatever she said, she had been looking forward to a great Gloomfest. But on the whole she was relieved, because, as she said, "I really don't like unhappy endings!" It is true: the end of

Thelma & Louise always reduces her to tears.

Anyway, I have decided... Carlito is going to live!!! With his manhood intact! He is coming out of hospital immediately and is going to have passionate love scenes of his own – only not in the heather. I am going to lie down in a minute and think of it.

Not having any episodes to read, we started talking about the two boys we met in Dandy's. Pilch had obviously got over her feelings of miffdom at Sean preferring me to her as she eagerly informed me that Tom reminds her of Alastair. I don't see the resemblance myself, apart from the fact that he has fair hair and goes to a posh school. (King Henry's. She says he asked her where she went, so she asked him in return. I didn't realise they had entered so deeply into conversation. It must have been while me and Sean were searching for Mum's album.)

"Don't you think he looks like Alastair?" she said.

I said yes, just to make her happy – anything to stop her being miffed! – but I have to say that if either of them looks like anyone, it is Sean who looks like Carlito. I know that he is probably of Irish descent, but he has this very dark, very thick, very glossy black hair, and this wild, unkempt, almost gypsyish air. I was surprised that Pilch didn't comment on it! But I guess she is too busy dreaming of Alastair.

I asked her if she felt turned on by him, and she crinkled her nose and rubbed at her forehead and pretended to think about it before finally admitting that well, maybe, just a little bit.

"Be more precise!" I said. "What was the Tingle Factor?"

This made her rub even more furiously at her forehead.

"Mm… about… nine?" she said.

She calls that a little bit??? Fortunately she didn't ask me about Sean as I am not at all sure what I would have answered!

We have agreed that we will go in again next Saturday and check whether Mum's album has turned up.

Sunday

Woke to the sound of strange noises coming from Mum's bedroom. Well, Mum and Harry's bedroom as it is now. Strange thuddings and thumps. I thought at first it was a burglar, tripping over the edge of the rug and banging his head against the chest of drawers. I knew Mum was downstairs because I could hear her warbling to herself in the kitchen. (She does a lot of warbling, these days. A sign, I suppose, that she is happy.)

So, anyway, I crept out of my room, all prepared to do battle – or more likely shriek my head off, as at heart I am a coward – and what did I see, through the open door? Harry is what I saw! Harry, trying to get into his underpants…

He'd got one leg in OK but seemed to be having problems with the other. Every time he tried to put his foot through the leg hole, which is certainly big enough, I mean it's leg-sized, for God's sake! Well, every time he tried, he kept catching his toe in the waistband, losing his balance and hopping about on his other leg. (Hence all the thuddings and thumps.) Every time it happened he shouted 'Ollocks!' It was like some mad kind of song and dance.

Jab – thud! – Ollocks! – Jab – thud! – Ollocks!

I stood silently watching in the doorway. I thought to myself, this is my mum's boyfriend, the man who could well become my stepfather, and he cannot even get into his own underpants!

And then I thought of Mum, who had got into her jeans and couldn't get out, and I thought that maybe this was a sign they were made for each other and could grow old and silly together. I mean, more silly than they are already! I pictured them holding up the queue at supermarket check-outs as they fumbled for their money, and doddering snail-like across the road in the path of juggernauts, causing all the traffic to screech to a halt and being blissfully unaware of it. Rather touching, really.

I didn't wait to see if Harry made it into his underpants but assume he did as the shouting finally stopped and so did the thudding.

Spent most of the day working on a new episode. It is rather steamy… definitely Tingle Factor!!! About ten plus.

Must remember to buy a birthday card for Mum, and some wrapping paper for her prezzie.

Monday

(6th Week)

Pilch asked me something interesting today. She asked me if I thought that Alastair and Carlito would still be with us when we are old and grey, and if so whether they would also be old and grey. I mean, will they grow up along with us, or will they remain for ever young and beautiful?

Pilch says young and beautiful, but I am not sure. I

have noticed with Mum, when we watch videos together, it is always the older men she fancies. Well, not the very old ones, such as for example Paul Newman or Clint Eastwood. They are too old even for Mum! But ones that I would consider old, such as... I am trying to think of some. Mel Gibson! That is one. Harrison Ford. That is another. I am sure they were quite dishy in their time, but to me they are middle-aged and therefore past their sell-by date. Sexually speaking, so to speak. No Tingle Factor. I mean, jowls are not a turn-on!

Mum, however, will look at someone young and will dismiss him, saying, "He's nice, but he's just a boy." Like for her a boy has no attraction. Which is just as well, when I think of Harry! Harry not only has jowls, he has the beginnings of a paunch. I mean, he is nearly forty!

What I'm trying to say, which is what I tried to say to Pilch before we were extremely rudely interrupted, is that maybe as we grow older our dreams will grow older with us. Except that I never got around to explaining it properly as that tiresome duo, Cindy and Tasha, suddenly materialised out of absolutely nowhere and started mindlessly burbling at us.

Cindy cried, "Honestly! You two are so weird. What

on earth do you find to talk about all the time?"

To which I smartly retorted, "Wouldn't you like to know?"

"Well, since you ask," said Cindy, "yes!"

"Go on, do tell," said Tasha.

A brilliant riposte then came to me. I opened my mouth intending to utter the following piece of scintillating sarcasm:

"We happen to have been discussing Einstein's Theory of Relativity, if that means anything to you."

Which would have put them in their place for sure, since they have almost certainly never even heard of Einstein, let alone his Theory of Relativity. Pilch, however (she can be very quick off the mark) got in before me.

"We were talking about men," she said, "if you must know."

Quick off the mark she may be, but Pilch does not always think before she speaks. The two morons promptly went into gales of stupid laughter.

"Men!" spluttered Tasha.

"What would you know about them?" gasped Cindy.

At this I suddenly lost all control and shouted, "Sibtupid miborons!"

I have been longing to say that to them. And now I

have done it! What is more, it shut them up. I could see them wondering to themselves, is this some kind of an insult? And what language is she speaking? Me and Pilch just put our noses in the air and stalked off, leaving them standing there. Pilch said, "Hey! We haven't used IBBY for years!"

I said, "I know it's childish, but it gave me great satisfaction."

Whereupon Pilch instantly turned round and thumbed her nose, which no doubt gave her great satisfaction. They get you like that, those two.

Tuesday

My cup runneth over! Mrs Adey called me up at the end of English. She said, "Your work has been really excellent this term, Cresta. I'm extremely pleased with you!"

If there is anyone on this earth who I want to be pleased with me, it is Mrs Adey. It somehow makes the whole unequal struggle worthwhile.

When I say unequal struggle, I am referring to:

a) life in general (the constant nagging worry about whether the world is going to come to an end through pollution, global warming, etc.), b) certain aspects of life in particular (Mum nagging at me springs immediately to mind) and c) still being less than half way through *War and Peace*.

Well, not even a quarter of the way, if I am to be strictly honest, and I suppose there's not much to be gained from lying to myself. I wouldn't say that I'm finding it drags, exactly, it is far too fine and noble for that; but it does have a tendency to be what I should call long-winded.

I shall, however, go back to it in the holidays.

This I SOLEMNLY SWEAR.

Wonders will never cease! First Mrs Adey, now Mum. All of a sudden, it seems, I am flavour of the month. Long may it continue!!!

Tonight, as we sat down to tea, Mum said, "I stopped off at Tesco's on the way home. I bumped into Mrs Sullivan."

Brad Sullivan's mum. I thought, "Uh-oh!" and braced

myself for yet another onslaught. Instead...

"How that woman does go on!" said Mum.

I said, "Really?" perking up a bit. "What does she go on about?"

"Oh, how the sun shines out of her precious son's you-know-what," said Mum.

I almost giggled at this. Why can't she just say the word, like everyone else? She's funny about language, is Mum. Which is strange, when you think about it... with Harry around the place!

"He's a nice enough boy," said Mum. "I have nothing against him. I just don't particularly want an ear bashing over the frozen foods about what a genius he is!"

"He can't be much of a genius," I said. "Not going out with Tasha Lansmann."

"Tasha Lansmann? The little redhead?" said Mum. Mum always remembers what people look like. "Very attractive!"

"She's a moron," I said. You couldn't get much dumber than Tasha. Well, not unless you happened to be Cindy. Tasha's a moron, Cindy is brain-dead.

Mum said, "It's often the way... you trade on your looks and let the rest go to pot. I know!" She pulled a face. "I've been there." And then she said this thing which really surprised me. She said, "Fortunately you've got more sense. You've inherited my looks, but not my dizziness."

Wow! Does she mean I'm pretty???

Have just stopped to gaze soulfully at myself in the mirror. I do have a nice nose! I think. But must not get hung up on looks. Don't wish to become like Tasha!

I said to Mum, since she seemed to be in an unusually receptive mood, that I aimed to make work my absolute A1 priority until I had taken my A levels and got to uni.

"Very sensible," said Mum.

What has come over her? Thinks: maybe Nan has said something? Something about me being immature? Hm! Not sure I like that.

"Anyway, I gave her something to chew on," said Mum, meaning Mrs Sullivan. "I told her how you'd got an A* for your essay. That took the wind out of her sails!"

Phew! It's taken them out of mine, too! I mean, Mum… boasting about my essay! I never thought she cared.

It just goes to show, you should never judge people too hastily.

Thursday

After my recent triumphs with Mum and Mrs Adey, I today got my comeuppance (or put downance). Mr Bunting gave us our geography homework back. This is the homework I didn't do when I should have done so had to cram in while sitting on the bus. As a consequence, I have to admit, it was somewhat scrappy. Just a few scribbled lines plus a map gone wobbly. In his illiterate way, at the foot of the page, Mr Bunting had written, "Cresta McMorris did you really expect to get away with this? Come and see me after class."

He should, of course, have put a comma after my name, but commas evidently do not fall into his sphere of knowledge. Just as maps do not happen to fall into mine, which you would think, from the way in which he raged and frothed and generally carried on, was some kind of personal insult. Boy, oh boy! (Or Hombre! as Sean would say.) Is that man ever touchy?

Gloomed to Pilch about it as we went for our daily keep-fit tramp round the field, as far out of sight of the moronic duo as it was possible to get. Pilch, in her sensible way, said, "Why worry?" As she pointed out, since I cannot even follow a normal street map without getting lost, there hardly seems much point my trying to decipher contours and the like.

This is so true! I am notorious for having no sense of direction. If ever I am on a train, like for instance when we go and visit Nan, and I need the loo, I always have to make this mental note "When you come out, turn left" (or right, as the case may be) otherwise I would go gaily marching off the wrong way and wonder what had happened to all my stuff, and Mum. This being the case, I really don't see why Mr Bunting should take it so personally if my contours are wobbly.

"In any case," as Pilch said, "you're in with Mrs Adey." Meaning, I guess, why bother with boring Bunting? Hooray for Pilch! She has this knack of putting things into their proper perspective. I cheered up immediately.

"What did she want to speak to you about, anyway?" said Pilch.

Airily I said, "Oh! Nothing special." I didn't like to tell her what Mrs Adey actually said for fear it might sound like boasting. I hate people who boast!

I think I might tell Mum about it, though. Now I know that she is interested.

Spent the whole of PSE having thoughts about Carlito (brought on, I suspect, by Mrs Pink talking about birth control). It is amazing how the things that go on in your head can seem far more real than the things that are actually happening all around you. It is almost like living in another – and far more exciting! – dimension. Like sometimes in the morning, if I am in the middle of a daydream and Mum yells at me to get up or I will be late for school, it is really difficult, trying to drag myself back into the everyday world. I suppose this is what comes of having a vivid imagination.

Without realising what I was doing I decorated the front of my rough book with the name Carlito in flowery letters, with hearts and swirls.

Very arty! Unfortunately, however, at the end of the class the brain-dead half of the moronic duo caught sight of it.

"Ooooh!" she goes. "And who's Carlito?"

I said, "Wouldn't you like to know?" snatching up my rough book and shoving it into my bag.

"Is he your boyfriend?" said Tasha.

"Boyfriend?" shrieked Cindy. "She hasn't got a boyfriend! She wouldn't know what to do with a boy if she was handed one on a plate!"

That girl sucks.

Pilch came up to me afterwards and said, "You should have told her that he was!"

Pilch is right. I should have done!

Mum said today, as I was setting off to meet Pilch, "Wow! Aren't we looking smart!"

I don't know why she said that. I was only wearing quite ordinary stuff out of my wardrobe. My fitted shirt I got last Christmas, and my (mock) leather mini which I've had for ages. Oh, and the spider web tights that were Pilch's only she said her thighs bulged through them so she gave them to me. It was the first time I've worn them.

"Really nice," said Mum.

I was glad to have her approval, but it wasn't as if I'd got dressed up specially or anything. I mean, why should I? I was only going to meet Pilch!

First, before anything else, we went into Dandy's to see if Mum's record might have materialised. Sean was there. Also Tom. Sean said, "I don't think we've had any more Dawn of Humanity come in, but it's always worth going to have a look."

So we went up to the third floor, leaving Pilch downstairs on this occasion, and we looked through stacks and stacks, but all there was was an album called Lily Raven which Mum already has. I recognised the picture on the front, of this girl's face, pale green surrounded by water lilies.

"Brilliant, isn't it?" said Sean.

I agreed that it was, and as soon as I got home I took out Mum's copy and studied it, and he is right, it is quite amazing! This face, floating on its bed of lilies. It hadn't struck me before, for the simple reason that I hadn't bothered to look at it properly. I think sometimes you need a person to draw your attention to these things.

Sean said, "It's a bit like a painting they've got in the

Tate Modern," at which I immediately flew into a panic. I thought, Tate Modern, Tate Modern? Help, help! What is he talking about?

And then I remembered that of course it's an art gallery, up in town. Phew! Relief! I do so hate to show my ignorance.

He asked me if I had ever been there and I regretfully shook my head as there is no earthly use pretending you have done something if you haven't. It is far too easy to get caught out, and then I would just die.

Sean said that he had gone with his school, which turns out to be Halford Manor, where I could have gone if only Mum hadn't chosen all girls. Not that we would have been in the same class as Sean is in Year 10. He is sixteen! He asked me where I went and I said St Anne's and he said, "Oh! The Virgins!" He said that's what they call us as we all have to wear this excruciatingly gross uniform that I cannot imagine whoever could have dreamed up. I mean, purple pleated skirts and white blouses! At Halford Manor they wear whatever they like.

So we had a bit of a chat about our respective schools and Sean then said it was time for his tea break so why didn't we go up to the fourth floor? Which we did, and sat and drank Cokes while he told me all about the Tate

Modern. The way he described it, it sounds really interesting and the sort of thing I would enjoy as it is not just dreary paintings like in most places but also films and sculptures and a great many strange and fascinating exhibits.

I know it is wrong to say that paintings are dreary but I always grow a bit bored of just walking round staring, it makes my eyes go funny for one thing, and for another I start to yawn. I feel that films and sculptures would be far more stimulating. I now want like crazy to go there! Next week would probably be a good time as we are on half term.

After we had been upstairs for about fifteen minutes, Pilch suddenly appeared.

"Oh! There you are," she said.

Fortunately by then it was the end of Sean's tea break so he would have had to go back to the shop in any case. I said to Pilch that I was sorry I hadn't told her where I was, but she didn't seem very put out. She said she had been quite happy talking to Tom. So that was all right!

We then came back here to have tea, and on the way Pilch told me about Tom and the things that he had said. The things that Tom said, according to Pilch, would practically fill a book! The Wisdom of Tom, by Charlotte Peake.

She still insists that he looks like Alastair. I don't contradict her as I am only too pleased that she is happy to stay and talk to him while I discuss music and art and things with Sean. From what I can make out she and Tom talked mostly about hang-gliding, a subject on which only yesterday the depths of her ignorance were so deep as to defy all attempts at measurement, whereas today, lo and behold! she is a positive mine of information. Hang-gliding is obviously going to be Alastair's next thing.

Query: will he make mad passionate love to Zara while he is doing it???

Suggested to Mum, as she is taking this week off (to coincide with half term) that we should go to the Tate Modern together.

Mum said, "The Tate what?"

"Tate Modern," I said. "It's an art gallery."

Mum said, "Art gallery?"

Honestly! You'd think I'd suggested a visit to a sewage farm, or something.

"What do you want to go to an art gallery for?"

"Someone told me it was interesting," I said.

"Full of bricks and poo," said Harry.

It is a terrible struggle, trying to get any culture in this house.

"It has films," I told Mum, "and sculptures. And a painting like on the front of one of your records."

Mum immediately said, "Which one?"

I took out Lily Raven and showed it to her. The girl amongst the water lilies.

"That's in there?" said Mum.

"Don't you believe it!" said Harry. "Bricks and poo. That's all you'll find."

He is a very coarse sort of man. I mean, I do like him, and he is quite fun and ever so good to Mum, but I cannot pretend that he is an intellectual. But then neither, of course, is Mum. She freely admits that she wasted her time at school by running after boys.

"Boys on the brain!" She actually said it.

Anyhow, she has agreed that tomorrow we will go for what she calls "our culture bash". Harry has said that he will drive us there.

"But that's it," he said. "That's as far as it goes! You two girls go in by yourselves. You don't get me paying good money to look at bricks and piles of poo!"

Monday

(7th Week)

Hah! Harry was wrong on both counts: we didn't have to pay anything to go in as it is completely free (unless you want to go to the special exhibitions, which we couldn't as by then Mum was getting restless and complaining of feet ache) and there weren't any piles of poo! Not that I could see. Not unless some of the things I thought were volcanic rocks were in fact petrified dinosaur turds, which I suppose they could have been.

Mum, I regret to say, was totally flippant. She didn't take it seriously at all. To her it was just one big joke. She kept making these idiotic comments such as, "Oh, look! Somebody's emptied a dustbin over the floor," or, "A load of old stones! How interesting."

It was really embarrassing, especially as there were a great many German and Japanese tourists eagerly pointing things out to one another and talking in knowledgeable tones about the various exhibits. My only comfort was that Harry had not come with us as he would have been a thousand times worse even than Mum. Who was quite bad enough!

Some of the exhibits, I must admit, were rather rude, but still I don't think Mum should have made the remarks that she did. There was one in particular, which I would just die rather than mention to Sean! Waggling Willies is the title I would give it. I mean that is what it was. Mum took one look and went, "Oh! The last Tory cabinet," which made a man standing nearby give a loud snort of laughter. When I asked Mum what she meant she just smirked and said, "Well, they couldn't keep their trousers up."

Honestly! In an art gallery.

There was another one that wasn't rude exactly, as it was very tastefully done, except that I am not sure that very young children could be allowed to watch it.

This was a film of two men, without any clothes on, sort of wrestling each other (amongst other things). You had to walk in a darkened tunnel to watch it, and I was quite glad that the lights were dim so that no one could see my face, because as usual I lit up like a beacon. This is so puerile of me. The human form is nothing to be ashamed of.

Actually, it was Mum I was ashamed of. In this loud and scoffing tone of voice she said, "Well! Whatever turns you on." I could have died. I mean, everyone else, all the Germans and the Japanese, were standing there watching in postures of immense seriousness. All I could hope was that perhaps they might think Mum's expression had been one of artistic appreciation.

I do not pretend to have understood everything we saw today but at least I tried, which is more than Mum did. The things on which she poured her scorn are actually quite challenging, as they make you think. You ask yourself, what is it, and why, and what does it mean?

Harry, when I told him this, said, "And what do you answer yourself?"

But he was not being serious. He never is.

I am quite cross with Harry, as a matter of fact. I am cross with both of them. I have come to the conclusion that I live with Philistines.

When we got home, Harry was already here. He is taking time off to be with Mum and is going to be here the whole week, which ordinarily I wouldn't mind as I quite like having him about the place, but not if he is going to make fun of me. We never managed to find Sean's water lily painting on account of Mum having had enough and wanting to come home, but I did find a postcard of it and also bought some other postcards to remind me of our visit. I showed the cards to Harry, mistakenly thinking he would be impressed, but after holding them at all silly angles, both upside down and sideways, and squinting first with one eye and then the other, all he could find to say was, "Call this art?"

Considerably annoyed I retorted, "What would you call it?"

Harry said "Me?" and gave one of his coarse guffaws. "I'd call it more like fart!"

Mum then told him about the waggling willies and Harry said, "Well, stone me! I'll waggle my willy any time you like."

Oh, yes? And who does he think would want to see his saggy old parts?

Tuesday

Went round to see Pilch. Found her fretting at herself with a tape measure, saying once again that she is too fat.

I said, "What's brought this on? I thought you'd got over all that nonsense."

Pilch said, "It's not nonsense. Look at me!" And she seized great handfuls of her flesh and squeezed. "Ugh! It's revolting!"

I said, "It is not revolting, it just happens to be the way that you are made." Like she has curly hair and freckles and a tip-tilty nose. I said, "It's what nature has programmed you for."

Pilch said, "Well, in that case I am going to deprogramme myself! Starting as of right now!" And she angrily waved away the bar of KitKat that I had brought for her.

I think it is very sad that someone of Pilch's intelligence should allow herself to be pressurised into changing the natural shape of her body. But it is no use my saying anything. She actually watched me eat my way through two bars of KitKat. She wasn't even tempted when I held out the last finger. This is serious! I have never known Pilch not be tempted by a KitKat before. Cheese, of course, will be the real test.

She asked me, while I was munching, what I did yesterday, and I told her about going to the Tate Modern and Mum's ridiculous behaviour. I also told her about Harry and his crude scoffing. I said, "He is not at all a cultured kind of person. In fact he is quite coarse," and I gave her the story of the underpants.

Pilch listened in wide-eyed silence. At the end she said, "Did you see anything?"

I said, "What do you mean, did I see anything? I saw

his big hairy bum, if that is what you mean."

"Oh, you mean he had his back to you," said Pilch.

I said, "Yes, and I saw his bum cheeks pobbling up and down every time he tried to get his foot in."

"Like this?"

Pilch jumped up, giggling, and began to mime being Harry.

"Oops! Ollocks. Oops! Ollocks."

I said, "It's not very funny, Mum having a boyfriend who can't even manage to get into his own underpants."

"I think it is," giggled Pilch, hopping about on one leg. "Oops! Ollocks. Missed again!"

I didn't want to laugh, but I just couldn't help it. It ended up with us both hopping round the room going oops ollocks.

We have agreed to meet up tomorrow and go to Dandy's. Mum's record might just have come in! As Pilch said, "You wouldn't want to miss it."

I know they have our telephone numbers, but these things can easily be mislaid.

Wednesday

Went into Dandy's but Sean wasn't there. And to think I spent ages looking through my scanty and meagre wardrobe for something to put on. Not that I believe clothes to be that important, I mean personally I would be quite happy if everybody wore jeans, but until that happens it is a case of having to find the right clothes for the right occasion, which can be somewhat bothersome as well as time-consuming.

Thought: why can't we have fur like animals? It would solve all our problems! Bare skin is really not practical.

Tom was there and I had to listen to a long and dreary conversation between him and Pilch about hang-gliding, as sure enough Pilch has been to the library and found one of her famous books, How To Hang-Glide in a Thousand Easy Lessons, or some such thing. After a while I grew bored and wandered upstairs to look through the records, but it wasn't such fun doing it on my own, without Sean to talk to, especially as they were all the same ones that I'd looked through last time. So I went back down to the ground floor to find that Tom and Pilch were still at it. Can hang-gliding really be that fascinating???

I didn't like to ask where Sean was in case it seemed like I'd only gone there in the hope of seeing him, rather than to look for Mum's record, but fortunately Tom told me anyway. He said, "Sean's at the dentist. He'll be here after lunch."

Oh! It is so annoying. I couldn't go back after lunch as I had faithfully faithfully promised Mum that I would help with the decorating. Harry is doing the ceilings while me and Mum do the walls. Mum bribed me by saying in wistful tones that she really would love the place to look nice for her birthday. If you ask me, that is emotional blackmail! But there was no way I could wriggle out of it, especially after she came with me on Monday. Even if she did embarrass me by her behaviour. I know she doesn't do it on purpose. Embarrass me, I mean. She just doesn't know any better.

Pilch rang up this morning in a bit of a state to tell me that one of her boobs was bigger than the other.

I said, "How much bigger?"

Pilch said, "One and a half centimetres" if you took the tape measure up one side and down the other.

One and a half centimetres didn't sound like a whole lot to me but she had obviously worked herself into a state about it, thinking it was some kind of hideous deformity that was going to blight her entire existence. I said soothingly that I would go round and look as soon as I'd finished painting the sitting-room wall.

"How long will that take?" said Pilch.

I said, "Not long. Don't worry! They might have grown the same size by the time I'm through."

"It's not funny," moaned Pilch. "I'm unbalanced!"

Oh, dear! How she does exaggerate. It's like the time she pulled on her hooded top back to front and screamed that she'd gone blind. I thought she was joking, but she assured me afterwards that it had been a nasty moment... "Everything suddenly went dark!" She really gets stressed. I think she is prone to be a bit neurotic.

However, you can't leave your best friend to suffer agonies so immediately after lunch I went whizzing round to see what I could do.

"Right," I said, when the bedroom door was safely barricaded against invasion by tweenies. "What exactly is the problem?"

"I told you!" wailed Pilch. "My right boob is bigger than my left one!"

Quite honestly they both looked the same size to me, but Pilch insisted on getting out her tape measure and proving irrefutably (a good word!) that there was almost a centimetre and a half difference.

"It's not as if anyone would notice," I said.

Pilch said, "Not at the moment, maybe! But what if they grow?"

I told her that they would grow "in proportion" but she refused to be comforted. She kept saying that it was abnormal and that she was a freak and would never be able to go topless sunbathing.

"Topless sunbathing's bad for you anyway," I said.

Pilch yelled. "That's not the point! How would you like it if you were a freak?"

I said, "Well, for all I know I might be. I just don't go round measuring myself."

"Probably because you haven't got anything to measure," said Pilch.

This happens to be true, but I do think it was uncalled for. Pilch, to be fair, was immediately contrite. She said, "Oh, Pilch, I'm sorry! You can't help being flat chested."

I said, "I am not totally flat. I think something may be happening."

"Really?" said Pilch, and she walked round, eyeing me critically from every angle. "Well! I don't think you'll ever be a Marilyn Monroe," she said.

I know that. I take after Mum, who is skinny as a rail. Pilch said, however, that I should not despair.

"There are things you can do. I read in this book… *A Hundred Ways to Boost your Bust*. There are all these exercises. They probably wouldn't ever turn you into a D cup – " here she had the nerve to giggle "– but it might give you something to put in a bra!"

That did it. Loftily I informed her that I was quite happy for my bosom to develop as nature had intended, thank you very much.

"Oh, well, yes, of course," gushed Pilch, obviously realising she had offended me with her ill-mannered tittering. "I wasn't suggesting – I mean! Who cares anyway? It's not as if – well! I mean! At least," she said kindly, "you are not lopsided."

Generously, in the circumstances – though she had apologised, sort of – I said, "But at least you have a figure."

"I'm fat," said Pilch.

Of course I told her that she wasn't, which I don't think she is, I mean plump is not the same as fat, but she still insisted that she was.

She said, "I'm fat and I've got odd boobs!"

And then she told me how she'd been looking through this paper that her dad takes and they had a page called Mix 'n Match where people that want to meet other people (usually members of the opposite sex) send in photographs of themselves and say what sort of person they would like to meet up with.

"There was this one woman," said Pilch, "underneath her photograph she'd written that she had huge gravity-defying knockers."

"Did she?" I said.

"Yes! Enormous," said Pilch. "Out here!" And she made big balloon shapes in front of her.

I said, "I wonder how she kept them up?"

"Well, they were gravity-defying," said Pilch, which brought on a fit of infantile snickering from both of us.

We ended up standing side by side in front of Pilch's wardrobe mirror, comparing our shapes. We have never done this before! It was quite instructive. These are the conclusions we came to: I am more élégante, but Pilch is more cuddly. As to which of us is the more sexy, well! We agreed that this would depend on what a person is looking for.

One man's meat is another man's poison.

Anyway, she seems to have stopped worrying about her boobs being different sizes, so I feel I have fulfilled my duties as a friend.

We are going to meet in town tomorrow and go to

Dandy's as it is Mum's birthday on Saturday and this will be my last chance to find her album! If I could find it I would give her the two, and then I could go and look for another one for Christmas!

I have a horrid feeling I may be developing another spot as I have this great red blodge on my chin. I have smothered it in tea tree oil, which you are supposed to dilute but I didn't. I thought it might be more effective if I used it full strength. At the moment it is stinging like crazy, but I am not going to touch it! I have made this vow: I WILL NOT PICK. It is purely a matter of willpower.

Pulled out the whole of my wardrobe and fell into a state of total despair. I have absolutely nothing that is worth wearing! Ended up – as usual – putting on a pair of jeans. Over the top I wore my red bomber jacket with (fake!) fur collar, an outfit that always makes me feel butch, so to counteract the butchness I nipped into Mum's room and snitched a snazzy hat that she has, high-crowned with a floppy brim.

Mum, fortunately, was out shopping with Harry. Not that she would have minded me wearing her hat but I just didn't want any of her embarrassing remarks. "Oh yes, and who are you going to meet? The Queen?" That kind of stuff. It curls me up! I could hardly say that I was attempting to look half-way decent in the hope that Sean would keep a watch out for her album for her Christmas present. I mean, it would defeat the whole object of the exercise. It is supposed to be a secret!

Pilch was bad enough. "Oh! Groovy!" she said, casting an eye over Mum's hat. She could talk! I noticed that she was wearing make-up, which is a thing she normally never bothers with. It made me immediately wish that I had done the same, as my chin when I woke up this morning was glowing bright red like a beacon. Felt very self-conscious about it, though Pilch assured me it wasn't anywhere near as bad as I thought. All very well for her! But I know she meant well.

Went into Dandy's and Sean was there! He said that Mum's record had still not come in, but he suggested we went upstairs anyway, as it was, quite coincidentally, almost time for his break.

Tom had just had his, so Pilch stayed on the ground floor while Sean and I went up to the fourth, where he bought me a Coke and we shared a packet of crisps. He told me about his visit to the dentist and in return I told him about my visit to the Tate Modern and how Mum had embarrassed me.

To my relief Sean said that his mum is just the same, and his dad as well. He said his dad is a football fanatic and thinks that art is poncy.

"So does Harry," I said; and I told him about more like fart than art, which made him laugh.

"But Mum was really terrible," I said. "I just wanted to dig a hole and bury myself!"

And then, before I knew it, I found myself telling him about the Waggling Willies. Not that I actually said waggling willies. I wasn't brave enough for that! What I actually said was "She kept making fun of everything, you know? Like that one that was like the last Tory Cabinet?"

Sean looked puzzled and said, "Last Tory Cabinet?"

"Couldn't keep their trousers up," I said. "Let everything hang out?"

And then he got it. He said, "Oh! That one!" and made these little waggling motions with a finger, so that I giggled and choked myself and got all hot and red and thought, "Why do I say these things if I am not mature enough to do so without blushing?

173

Pathetic! I am just pathetic.

We had come to the end of Sean's break and were about to go back downstairs when he suddenly said, "If you're not doing anything tomorrow night, I suppose you wouldn't like to come to a party? If you're not doing anything, that is."

I gulped, and went furiously red for the second time, and immediately stammered that unfortunately I couldn't as it was Mum's birthday and we were going out for a meal, which made Sean also go pink as probably he thought I was simply making an excuse. He muttered, "Not to worry, I just thought I'd ask." So then I felt dreadful because it is bad enough embarrassing yourself without embarrassing someone else as well.

As we made our way downstairs Sean told me how the party was being held in the shop and was to celebrate Dandy's quarter centenary. It was only then that I noticed the balloons, and the streamers, and the spray-canned message on one of the mirrors: 25 YEARS OLD ON SATURDAY! Sometimes I think that I am not very observant.

I said, "I would have loved to come! Honestly!"

Sean said that he should have asked me sooner, though even if he had it would still have been Mum's birthday.

Feeling glum and inadequate I went to collect Pilch, who was sprawled across the counter talking to Tom.

"Are you coming?" I said.

"Yes, I suppose so." She peeled herself away.

"See you tomorrow," said Tom.

"Tomorrow?" I said, as we got outside. "Are we coming in again tomorrow?"

"The party," said Pilch. "Didn't Sean ask you?"

"You mean, you're going?" I said.

Pilch said yes, she was.

"But we don't go to parties!" I said.

"Well, I'm going," said Pilch.

I stared at her in dismay. Me and Pilch don't do things separately! We don't make unilateral decisions. We consult. She couldn't go waltzing off to a party without me! Especially when it was my mum who was the reason for us going into Dandy's in the first place. If it hadn't been for that, she'd never even have been asked!

"I'm definitely going," said Pilch. "I mean, just because you don't like parties—"

But she doesn't, either! At least, that's what she's always said.

"Oh, look! This is ridiculous!" cried Pilch. "You know I can't go without you! Oh, come on, Pilch!

175

Please!" She jigged up and down on the pavement, clasping her hands in beseeching fashion. "Don't be boring!"

I yammered at her that it was Mum's birthday.

"But she's got Harry!" said Pilch. "Oh, please, please, please! Don't spoil things! It'll be ever such fun!"

I have never had fun at a party. Never. I am just so useless!

"Pilch, listen to me." Very firmly, she hooked her arm through mine, clamping me to her side. "I don't want to go on my own! We don't do things on our own. But I will go on my own! If I have to."

I stood there, dithering.

"I've already told Sean," I bleated.

Pilch said, "So go back and say that you've changed your mind!"

I looked at her, uncertainly. I couldn't believe this was happening!

"Listen! We have been asked," said Pilch, "to a party. And we are going to go. Right?"

I gulped and said, "R-right."

"So just get back in there!"

With that she gave me such a shove that I almost went flying headfirst through the door. I didn't even have a chance to think! I charged across the shop and gabbled, "You know I said I couldn't come tomorrow? Well I could always tell Mum I'm going to a party, I don't suppose she'd mind, she'd probably rather be on her own with Harry anyway."

I don't know how I found the courage! Suppose he'd said he'd already found someone else? Or that he'd changed his mind? I would just have shrivelled up and died! Right there and then, on the spot. But he seemed really pleased. Like he really does want me to go. Now I am both excited and looking forward to it with one part of me, and with another part I am dead nervous because suppose I end up in a corner, not talking? Sean will then wish he had never invited me and I will spend the evening praying for the earth to open up and swallow me and I will never dare go into Dandy's again. And we have been having *such* interesting conversations.

Apart from anything else, what am I going to wear???

Later:

Pilch rang to say that she had just read in a magazine how you could make a fab face mask by mashing up an overripe pear with half a teaspoon of honey and a dollop of double cream. She said, "I'm going to try it!" She said that I ought to try it as well, as it might help get rid of my spot.

I immediately charged downstairs to look in the fruit bowl. The only pear I could find was an avocado, and the only cream we have is tinned stuff, but I mashed it all up and sat here solemnly smothered in gunge for fifteen minutes (which is what Pilch said it takes) and am keeping my fingers crossed that it will work as I do not fancy the idea of going to party covered all over in spots!

Saturday

It did. It worked! The spot has disappeared! It is such a blessed boon to have a friend like Pilch. To know that we have each other's interests at heart and really do care.

Today was Mum's birthday, so over breakfast I gave her her prezzie. She was knocked out. She shrieked, "Oh, Cresta! This is one of the ones I've been looking for!" and immediately went rushing off to play it. Full volume, natch! But I didn't mind, as it's her birthday. I then had to break it to her that I wouldn't be going for a meal with her and Harry. Mum, when I had finished blurting things out, said, "Not coming with us? But why not?"

I muttered that I was going somewhere with Pilch. I didn't want to tell her that it was a party as I felt she might – not gloat, exactly, but be a bit triumphant. I mean, she has been nagging at me for ever about getting out and enjoying myself. Also I dreaded that she would start on about boys.

In the end, however, I was forced to explain that it was a birthday bash for Dandy's – "Where I got your record." Needless to say, her face at once broke into a big beam. She said, "Oh! A party. In that case, of course you must go! You don't want to be stuck with us when you could be out enjoying yourself."

i.e. Meeting boys. Mum is so transparent! But it is nice that she is pleased.

The party is starting at eight o'clock. Pilch's dad is very kindly going to take us there and bring us back again. He and Pilch are coming to pick me up in… two and a half hours' time! I am feeling all quivery inside.

Pilch came round this morning and instead of reading our latest episodes we discussed what we were going to wear tonight. I expect this may sound rather trivial, but as it happens I hadn't really got an episode as I have been too busy to do very much in the way of thinking. Pilch said she'd got a bit of one but had left it behind. She was more interested in asking me whether I thought she should wear trousers or whether trousers would make her bum look too big. She said, "It's all right for you! You haven't got any bum."

I am going to wear some fab gear that Mum has given me! A pair of boot leg trousers, black satin with red and silver embroidery, way too tight for Mum. She says, "I don't know why I ever bought them." I do! It was obviously so I could wear them to the party! She has also lent me her silver bangles and a silver necklace. It is good having a mum who can lend you trendy gear!

Pilch says that alas she wouldn't be seen dead in any of the stuff that her mum wears, but of course Pilch's mum is far older. I guess that is one of the advantages of having a mum who is still quite young!

Pilch still hadn't managed to come to any decision by the time she left. She said she was going to try on everything in her wardrobe and wear whatever is most flattering to her bum.

I am so glad I don't have bum problems!

A turning point in my life… I have been to a party! And I ENJOYED it!

Pilch and her dad called round at quarter to eight to pick me up. Pilch was wearing a crop top and shiny blue trousers! She said that since there was no way she could hide her curvy bits she had decided she might just as well advertise them.

"Like I am not going to be ashamed of my figure."

Well! This is a departure. And a very welcome one. I think it was a brave decision and the right one to have made. She looked dead sexy! She had painted sparkly stuff over her eyelids and sprayed it in her hair. I don't know where she has learnt to do these things. From her sister Janine, probably. Next time – if there is a next time! – I am going to be brave, like Pilch.

The party was held upstairs on the fourth floor. All the tables had been pushed back and there was food and drink that you could just help yourself to, and a DJ playing records from twenty-five years ago, including Lily Raven, which Sean said he requested specially for me!

Lots of people started dancing and for a moment I was in a panic, thinking I would have to run away and hide in the loo like I used to do in Juniors. I have always had this belief that I cannot dance. I am too self-conscious! But then I saw this really ancient couple going at it, and it gave me courage because quite honestly what on earth did they look like? He was wearing these baggy jeans and had long grey hair tied in a ponytail, whilst being totally bald on top, and she had this thin wrinkly neck like a tortoise and droopy old boobs that swung to and fro as she danced. And they just didn't care! So I thought that I wouldn't care, either, and before I knew it I found myself throwing caution to the wind and not bothering about who might be watching.

Cindy Williams was there! I was quite surprised to see her. She was probably even more surprised to see me. Especially in the company of Sean! It seems that her dad supplies the restaurant with cakes and stuff. Not very distinguished, I don't think. She did her best to elbow her way in, I just knew she was angling for Sean to dance with her, but he wouldn't! He stuck with me. A bit later she tried it on with Tom (Pilch told me this) but Tom wouldn't dance with her, either. That girl is too pushy by half! And anyway, she looked a total sight.

At eleven o'clock Pilch's dad came by to pick us up. The party was still in full swing. Some people had gone but new ones kept arriving, so Pilch's dad came upstairs and had a drink and then he saw someone he knew and started chatting, so that it was nearly midnight by the time we left. Pilch's dad is quite a jolly sort of person.

Mum and Harry, of course, were already home when I got back. Needless to say, they wanted to hear all about it! The party, I mean. I realise this is quite natural and only to be expected, but the fact is you don't always feel like sharing things with people. Sometimes you just want to hug them to yourself! Mum in particular was full of questions. Exactly the sort of questions I knew that she would ask! Such as, "Who was there?" and "Did you dance?" and "Who did you dance with?" etc. and so forth. Desperately trying to discover whether I had met a boy!

Dashing her hopes I said, "As a matter of fact, they were mostly pretty ancient."

This was probably a bit mean, as Mum immediately looked disappointed. She said, "No one your own age?"

I said, "Me and Pilch and one or two others. Plus a girl from school who we can't stand."

"Oh. Well! But you had a good time?" said Mum.

I said I had; and with that, I'm afraid, she had to be content!

Spent most of the night lying awake, with my brain all fizzing and bubbling. Didn't get up until nearly midday. Harry, who is rewiring the kitchen, said, "It's all right for some."

Longing to discuss things with Pilch but we agreed we would leave it till tomorrow, when we can be private. It is not safe to telephone. Walls have ears!

Later:

Talking of telephones... Mum just called me downstairs. She said, "There's someone asking for you." I couldn't think who it might be as I knew it couldn't be

Pilch and there is really no one else who would ring me.

"Some young man," said Mum, handing me the phone.

It was Sean!!! Wanting to know if I would go to the movies with him next Saturday. Of course I said that I would! He said, "I don't know what's on, but there's bound to be something."

I said that it didn't really matter what was on as I was a simply terrific movie buff and could sit through practically anything.

We have agreed that we will meet at Dandy's at six o'clock, which is when he gets off work. Now I am in an agony, wondering what to tell Pilch!

(8th Week)

Mum, needless to say, has been almost bursting at the seams with vulgar curiosity concerning my telephone call! She managed to contain herself until breakfast this morning, when all bright and casual she goes, "So who was that who rang you last night? Someone you met at the party?"

I have told her that it was "just a boy who works in the

shop". I suppose in the end I shall have to admit that we are going to the movies together. That is two people I have to break it to: Mum, and Pilch!

Pilch said to me today that she thinks we ought to stop calling each other by absurd and childish nicknames. She said that it is "not becoming" and that in future she is going to call me Cresta and she would like me to call her Charlie. I sort of agree with her, but it is going to be very difficult after all these years!

We talked about the party and about what a total fright Cindy had looked and how neither Sean nor Tom wanted anything to do with her, and Pilch, that is Charlie, told me that her dad had thought I looked "very grown-up". I said that personally I had felt boring and dowdy and that I was thinking of going into town some time to look for new clothes. Charlie said that she would come with me as two heads are better than one, so that is what we are going to do. On Thursday, which is late-night shopping. We shall shop till we drop and then have a pizza!

I haven't yet broken it to her that I am going to the movies with Sean on Saturday evening and won't be able to see her. Why does this make me feel so guilty? I suppose it is because we have been going round to each other's places on a Saturday for simply years, ever since we left Juniors. Pilch is bound to feel left out. But what can I do? There are some occasions when two is company and three is quite definitely a crowd!!!

Have just realised... I have written Pilch again instead of Charlie. This is going to take some getting used to!

Tuesday

I really hate that Cindy Williams. She came simpering up to me today and said, "How's your spotty boyfriend?" Sean is not spotty! He happened to have one little pimply patch on his chin, which I only noticed as I am somewhat sensitive about chins. But that does not make him spotty! I suppose she is just trying to denigrate him because she is jealous.

Still haven't told Pilch about Saturday. I mean Charlie.

Wednesday

It is no use! I cannot get used to calling Pilch by another name.

Went clothes shopping with Charlie. Am feeling so guilty about Saturday that I am now making a DETERMINED EFFORT to stop addressing her as Pilch. Charlie Charlie

Charlie! It seems the least I can do.

Was positively racked with guilt the entire time we were shopping. I kept thinking to myself, "She does not realise that I am planning to wear these garments on Saturday evening when I go out with Sean." So that is why I am making this big effort to dignify her with her given name and no longer refer to her as a fish.

These are the clothes I have bought:

A black ribby top (chosen by Pilch)

A yellow skirt (short as short, chosen by me!)

Black tights

I could not alas afford new shoes, but Pilch says my black ones with the kitten heel will go OK, and over the top I plan to wear my Levi jacket (unless it is freezing cold, which I fervently hope it is not as my only coat is dead naff and I should be ashamed to be seen in it).

Oh, I have done it again! Twice. How am I going to make myself remember???

Spent all day frantically wondering what I am going to tell Charlie about tomorrow – and when I am going to do it! It is a bit too late to say that Nan is coming, as I would have known about this ages ago since Nan never does anything on the spur of the moment. Although I could always perhaps say that I had forgotten?

But then there would be the problem, just suppose

Charlie took it into her head to ring me and Mum said that I was out??

It would be far better to tell her the truth but I am so afraid she will be hurt!

I still cannot decide.

A lot to report!

First off, I had to tell Mum that I was going to the movies with Sean. Instead of being thrilled into tiny little pieces by this news, she instantly set about giving me the third degree! Who was he, how had I met him, was he one of the ones that worked in the shop, what did I know about him, where did he live, where were we going, how old was he?

"I thought you said they were all ancient?" said Mum. "I don't want you going out with a thirty year old!"

I had to explain that Sean was only sixteen and still at school and just worked on Saturdays. This mollified her somewhat, but she still wanted to know where we were going and what time I was getting back.

"I want you in no later than eleven o'clock! And how do you propose to get here? You'd better take the mobile and give us a ring, then Harry can come and pick you up. I don't want you using public transport. Not at that time of night."

I said, "Mum, I'm quite capable of looking after myself!"

"You're fourteen," said Mum. "I'm not sure I should be letting you go at all."

I shrieked, "Mum!"

"You can Mum me as much as you like," she said. "Why can't you meet earlier?"

"Because he's working," I said.

"Well," said Mum, "you just make sure you take that phone. And where exactly are you going, anyway?"

I told her that we hadn't yet decided, so then she got in a fuss about that. Like she was having these visions of Sean kidnapping me and bearing me off to foreign parts to be a sex slave. Like he was some kind of drug-crazed pervert. I just could hardly believe it! This was my mum? Dizzy blonde, boys on the brain... Some people, it seems, are just never satisfied!

Anyway, she solved one of my problems by saying that if I was going out, she and Harry might as well go out, too. She said, "We'll be over at Tansy's. I'll give you the number, and you can ring us there."

I thought that this was providential (if that is the word) as it meant I could tell Charlie that I was also going to be at the Tansy person's, so I picked up the phone and Janine answered it and I said, "Hi, it's Cresta. Could I speak to Charlie?" feeling very pleased with myself that I had remembered to call her by her proper name. I heard Janine yelling up the stairs, "Charlie-it's-your-fish-friend!"

Charlie herself then came to the phone and said, "Pilch!"

Really, I ask myself! Why do I bother?

"This is Cresta," I said.

"Oh! Yes. Oops! Sorry! Cresta," gabbled Charlie. "Listen, I was going to ring you. You'll never guess what I've gone and done... I've gone and sprained my ankle! It's all wrapped up, I can't walk properly. Isn't it a bore?"

"Frightful," I said. "How did you do it?"

She said, "Oh, just tripped over. It means we won't be able to meet, boo hoo!"

I said, "Never mind. I hadn't got another episode, anyway."

She said, "No, neither had I."

There was then a bit of a pause.

"Hope your ankle gets better," I said.

"Oh, it will," she said. "It'll be all right by Monday."

So that was that! I felt hugely relieved.

Stayed home all day, washing my hair and practising make-up. I bought some glittery stuff on Thursday, same as Charlie had, but it doesn't seem to suit me like it does her. It must be the wrong colour, or something. I had to wash it all off again.

Finally got ready – "Home by eleven!" thundered Mum – and caught the bus into town. It seemed very strange to be going in at that hour and as a matter of fact I felt quite nervous. As a rule I would have had Charlie to keep me company but now I was on my own! However, as soon as I saw Sean I felt all right as he is one of those people, he puts you immediately at your ease. Plus we have so many things to talk about! School, and families, and books and paintings, not that I know very much about the latter, but I intend to learn. Things that have happened in the shop, movies that we have seen. The list is endless!

(Unlike with poor old Spooky Steve, who could only talk about his wretched hamsters.)

We discussed where we should go. Life in this town can be very frustrating for a teenager. We have only one cinema that shows current movies, and the movie they happened to be showing right now was an 18, which we didn't think, probably, we would be able to get into. It is so stupid! I watch them all the time at home. Well, sometimes I do. But we didn't want the ignomimy–nomony–? we didn't want to be *embarrassed* by being told we were under age so we went to the Re-Run House, instead, where they were showing something called Priscilla Queen of the Desert which is a 15 (but no problem!) and which we both thought was going to be really pukey, all about lurv, but which turned out to be truly wicked and amusing. It was about three men who dressed up as women and got to sing songs by Abba and travelled across the Australian outback in a bus painted pink. Mum, I know, would just love it!

Afterwards, when we had gone for a pizza, Sean seemed a bit worried about having laughed so much. He said, "I hope you don't think I'm gay? I'm not an Abba fan!"

I said, "Why? Are Abba fans gay?"

Sean said, "Well, there's got to be something wrong with them," which made me giggle (though actually I quite liked the Abba songs) but then suddenly he came over all serious and said, "Not that I'm saying there's anything wrong with being gay… just something wrong with being an Abba fan!" So that I was glad I hadn't admitted to liking them!

It is rather a minefield when you know so little about a subject – music, in my case – and cannot decide whether you should like a thing or whether it is dead naff. But I am learning!

We had just finished eating our pizzas when a rather strange incident occurred: Charlie went walking past! She was holding hands with Tom, and she wasn't even limping. I find this decidedly odd.

Sean has asked me if I will go to a party with him next Saturday!

This morning at eleven o'clock, Charlie rang. She said, "Is it OK if I come round?"

I said, "What about your ankle?"

"Oh," she said, "that's much better!"

I thought to myself, yes, it was much better last night, only I didn't say so as I didn't want unpleasantness. I know she lied to me, but I was going to lie to her, as well, so I was just as bad. Except that as it turns out we were both doing it with the best of intentions!

"I didn't want you to be upset," said Charlie.

I said, "I didn't want you to be!"

"I was scared you might feel, like… left out," said Charlie.

I said I was scared that was how she might have felt.

"The reason I came round," she said, "Tom's asked me if I'll go to a party with him next Saturday."

I said, "Sean's asked me if I'll go to one!"

At this we both broke out into relieved giggles.

"Oh!" said Charlie. "You don't think it's the same party?"

I think it probably is. I am so glad we don't have to lie to each other any more!

Three years later...

My long-lost diary! I thought it was gone for ever. I discovered it this morning, while clearing out my bedroom cupboard. I have been trying to re-read it, but I can't! It is just so embarrassing. What weird creatures we were! Both of us. Though I think if anything I was the weirder of the two. If it hadn't been for me, I don't believe that Charlie would have been weird at all. I was the one always going on about educating ourselves and reading the classics and not being side-tracked by boys.

I never did finish reading *War and Peace*. But there is still time! I have not given up on it. It is there on the shelf, with a bookmark stuck at page 412. I am not sure what happened after page 412. Boys, probably!

In those days it was Mum who had them on the brain. Now it is me! Not that I am obsessed, I think it is pathetic if female thoughts revolve solely round the opposite sex. But they can be quite interesting and amusing, and make a refreshing change from girly gossip. At any rate, I should not like to live in a world which did not contain them. In other words, I am not cut out to be a nun!!!

Nor is Charlie, that is for sure. She is going out with this gorgeous hunk called Josh that she met in Aquazoo, where she does Saturday work. I am going out with Craig, whom I met at a party. Me, at a party! But I go to them all the time these days. And I never stand in corners or hide in the loo! I have become terrifically normal.

It is so strange how things turn out. I blush now to remember how I used to have all those erotic day-dreams about Carlito. Charlie used to day-dream about Alastair (whom I secretly always thought was a bit of a wimp).

Alastair was the embodiment of worldly sophistication, where Carlito represented a primitive force. How we used to drool over them! (I dread to think what became of all the drivel I wrote. All those episodes! If ever I find them I shall immediately consign them to a black plastic bin bag. No power on earth would get me to read them again!)

What is strange is that it is Charlie who is now going out with a primitive force while I am going out with worldly sophistication. Craig is so cool!

I still see Sean from time to time. He is at uni, studying to become a doctor. We are good friends and hopefully always will be. Tom and Charlie, on the other hand, had this simply humungous row when Charlie caught Tom going out with another girl, so that for ages I hardly dared even mention his name. It made things a bit awkward, what with him and Sean being such good buddies, but she got over it in the end. These things happen.

The reason I have been tidying out my cupboard is that we are moving. After all this time! Mum and Harry got married last August, and now they have bought a house just a few blocks away. Mum is thrilled as it has a) a fitted kitchen and b) a spare bedroom. She has become tremendously staid! She complains that her waistline is spreading, though I have to say I cannot see any signs of it. She still looks really good for her age. But she and

Harry hardly ever go out on the razzle any more. They seem quite content just to stay in and watch the telly. And sometimes, at ten o'clock, they will say, "Let's go to bed and read." Sad, in a way; but nice that Mum is part of a Happy Couple!

Funny to think that it used to be me saying to Mum, "You can't go out like that!" and now it is Mum who says it to me. She said it only last night – well, shrieked it, actually.

"Cresta! You can't go out dressed like that!"

It was Harry who came to my rescue. He said, "Oh, let her be! She's young. She can get away with it."

Good old Harry! He is really quite a sweetie.

Even though we broke our vows of celibacy – no boys before uni. Oh, dear! Such nonsense – Charlie and I have not given up on our ambitions. We are still going to be brain surgeons! Or the equivalent of. Charlie is going to do marine biology and travel the world charting the oceans. (She got this idea from working in Aquazoo.) I am going to study law. I am going to become a lawyer! Or maybe a barrister. I have decided that one has to be practical, and quite honestly there doesn't seem to be enough money in just writing books. But I may still do it! I could write murder mysteries based on cases I have handled. They could then go on television and become best sellers, and I would be famous. Charlie could be famous by having her own programme, like David Attenborough, and talking about fish. Except these days I don't get the feeling that Charlie particularly hankers after fame. I do! I think. Just a little bit. But of course it is not the most important thing. Mum would say the most important thing is being happy, and I expect she is probably right.

I shall miss Charlie when we both go off to uni. We are bound to drift apart, it is almost inevitable. But it has to be said, we are not as close as we used to be. We used to be practically joined at the hip! One of us never did anything without the other. I can still remember the agonies I went through the first time Sean asked me out. How was I going to tell Charlie???

I do think boys tend to come between you. Josh and Craig, for instance, are like chalk and cheese and really do not get on at all, which makes going out as a foursome quite awkward. We have tried it a couple of times, but it really doesn't work.

I sometimes seriously wonder whether they ought to carry health warnings. Boys, I mean. The trouble is that once you've discovered them it's like BB and AB. Before Boys and After Boys. You can't imagine how you ever lived without them. They're kind of addictive, like smoking. Not that I do smoke, and I won't ever. I don't want to get lung cancer, thank you very much! At least boys don't do that. They just disturb the balance of your mind!!!

Oh! The bell has rung. That will be Craig, come to pick me up. We are going to a party! I must stop.

Goodness only knows how I ever found time to keep a diary! But that was BB. Life AB is far more hectic!

Mum has just called up the stairs. "Cresta, Craig is here!" Yes, yes, I'm coming. Farewell, sweet diary! Been nice knowing you.